Paige fell into Matt's arms and together they toppled onto the bed. Further ceremony was forgotten as he hurriedly peeled off her bikini panties and his own briefs, and any thought of restraint was cast aside with the last of their clothing.

Their limbs entwined and they lay tangled together, touching and kissing and tasting, tantalizing each other with hands and lips and tongues as their explorations became more and more intimate.

Matt moved over her, his body hard, hot, and possessive. "Have you any idea," he murmured, "how many times I've dreamed of this moment—dreamed you were with me like this, asking me to make love to you?"

ABOUT THE AUTHOR

Robin Francis read hundreds of romances before attempting to write one herself, and began working on her first book during the 1979 baseball World Series. Robin found her new hobby addictive and has been publishing romances ever since. This is her first Harlequin American Romance.

Memories of Love

ROBIN FRANCIS

Harlequin Books

TORONTO • NEW YORK • LONDON
AMSTERDAM • PARIS • SYDNEY • HAMBURG
STOCKHOLM • ATHENS • TOKYO • MILAN

Published January 1984

First printing November 1983

ISBN 0-373-16038-0

Prologue

Matthew Jonas didn't believe in good-byes. He'd done a fair amount of traveling in his thirty-five years, and he'd run into some of the most unlikely people in some of the least likely places. Just within the last six months he'd chanced to meet a boyhood chum in Beirut, his college journalism professor in Johannesburg, and a retired clergyman, who'd been one of his grandfather's cronies, in Corfu, so while he had good reason not to believe in good-byes, what he did believe was that the airport of nearly any major city provided a window on the world.

Matt was, first and foremost, a realist, but he knew with a certainty that bordered on the mystical that if a man cared to spend enough time in any large airport, he would see virtually everyone he'd ever known.

Because of this conviction, he shouldn't have been surprised when he saw Paige Cavanaugh at San Francisco's International Airport, but he was. In fact, to say that he was surprised was an understatement. Astounded was more like it. He was amazed, stunned, shaken.

They were separated by crowds of people and the full length of the baggage claim area, and although the fluorescent lighting in the terminal was harsh and glaring, it was certainly bright enough for him to make a positive identification. But finally, he was disbelieving.

As he jostled through the crowd, heading toward the United Airlines' baggage carousel, Matt shook his head impatiently to clear it, and this caused him to lose sight of the woman who resembled Paige. In the moments it took him to find her again, he questioned the reliability of his own senses.

He'd slept a total of six hours, maximum, in the last forty-eight. He'd just flown in from London, with a stopover in Washington, D.C. for a brief but boozy reunion with his friend Joe Hutchison. Not only did he have a monster hangover, he also felt as if he'd contracted terminal jet lag.

Furthermore, it had been a long time since he'd seen Paige. Almost eight years. And in those years there had been other women. It had taken him awhile to figure out that quantity was no substitute for quality, so for the first year or two, there had been too many women. But none like Paige. None of them had even come close.

And since he'd been looking for a Paige-replacement, it was understandable that there had been other occasions when he'd thought he'd seen her, then discovered he was mistaken. He could very well be mistaken now, but whoever this woman was, she looked enough like Paige to be her twin.

So where the hell was she?

When he was unable to locate her, Matt muttered a curse beneath his breath, which earned him a disapproving glare from the matronly lady nearest him. Matt smiled at her as she bustled past, but he didn't apologize, for in that instant he spotted the woman who resembled Paige again.

She was still standing near the Pacific Southwest Airlines' baggage carousel at the far end of the terminal, but she was no longer surrounded by people, and now that he had an unrestricted view of her, Matt was sure that she was Paige.

She had to be. The hair was a dead giveaway, and this woman's hair, like Paige's, fell to her shoulders in a silky spill of rich dark brown that was shot with red or gold, depending on the light. No two women could possibly have such glorious, glossy chestnut-colored hair.

Even from a distance, though, Matt could see that Paige had changed. She'd always had an air of gentle vulnerability, a softness, a delicacy that had made him intensely aware of her femininity. When he was with her he'd felt big and coarse and rawboned and, at the same time, powerfully masculine and fiercely protective.

To his dismay, Matt realized he still felt that way. The only difference was that now the urge to protect Paige was even more overwhelming because there was a new aura of fragility about her.

Perhaps this was an illusion, or perhaps she seemed

more fragile because her features were better defined than they had been when she was eighteen. The curve of her brow and cheek and jaw were more finely drawn.

As his appreciative glance roved over her body, Matt decided that her figure was better defined too. She was wearing a dark blue dress with a matching boxy jacket that concealed most of her curves, but his guess was that her breasts were fuller and her waist smaller. She was, he thought, more mature—more womanly. When his glance moved lower he saw that her hips still weren't very wide, but when she was eighteen, they'd been practically nonexistent. And her legs—they were the same; long and slender, sleek and beautifully proportioned.

He noticed that she was wearing shoes with three-inch heels, and he thought that this accounted for his impression that she was taller than he'd recalled.

He looked at her face once again. The way she was tipping her head back as if she were searching for someone in the crowd made her look almost regal. Without question, she was much more poised. She appeared to be utterly composed and completely self-possessed. But if she seemed aloof, she was also much more solemn than he'd remembered.

What had happened to Paige to make her so solemn? he wondered. And when had the transformation taken place?

He remembered her as being unguarded, ingenuous, smiling. He remembered her as being impulsive, and sometimes a bit self-conscious about her spontaneity. She might have been reserved with others, but never with him.

Paige had been an oddly unsophisticated eighteen-year-old. She'd been so damnably, touchingly young, and he'd been afraid of hurting her. But in the end, for all his caution, he supposed he had.

Paige had hurt him as well, of course, and what made it worse was that she'd inflicted the hurt without ever being conscious of her power over him.

Matt had few illusions about anything and almost none about women, but it wasn't until he'd recovered from the initial bitter disappointment that it had occurred to him to wonder whether Paige's apparent lack of guile could have been a pretense. Finally he'd concluded that she probably hadn't known how much he cared for her.

"After all," he'd reminded himself, "the young are notoriously self-centered." He'd told himself he shouldn't have expected a woman as inexperienced as Paige had been to have much insight into his feelings. She simply hadn't appreciated the damage she could do. And Lord knew there'd been a time when he'd been guilty of the same degree of insensitivity.

Until his experience with Paige, Matt had been accused of breaking more than a few hearts himself. Since then, however, he'd been very careful to keep his involvements light. He'd made it clear to the women he dated that he was interested only in short-term relationships. He made no secret of the fact that he wanted nothing more than a little fun, a few laughs, and no strings.

Matt thought he'd learned his lesson, but now he knew he hadn't.

Just watching Paige across the crowded baggage-claim area was exquisite torture. All he had to do was look at her and he could feel the silky texture of her hair between his fingers. He could smell the subtle lily-of-the-valley fragrance of her skin. His chest felt tight with passion and he ached to touch her.

Sweet Heaven! His hands were actually shaking.

Simmer down, Jonas, Matt told himself. He was behaving like a sex-starved schoolboy, standing there with sweaty palms, gawking at Paige when what he should do was walk over to her and say hello.

And then what? the skeptic in him demanded.

I'll follow up with something casual, Matt argued silently. *I'll say something friendly but nonincriminating. Something like, "Pardon me, but haven't we met somewhere before? Aren't you Paige Cavanaugh, the girl I used to call Irish?"*

Horsefeathers! the skeptic retorted, obviously not convinced he intended only to revive an old friendship.

But Matt refused to listen to the inner voice. He had started moving through the crowd toward Paige before he realized that she was no longer alone.

A man had joined her. A stocky, sandy-haired man who took her in his arms as if they'd been meeting at airports for years, as if he had every right to hold her, as if she belonged in his arms.

Matt recognized the man also. Jay Lowndes, he thought. One of Paige's old boyfriends from Stanford. And the irony was, Matt was the damn fool who'd persuaded Paige to go out with Jay in the first place!

The way Jay kissed Paige now was not really lover-like. It was more as if he were comforting her. But there was an easy familiarity between them that seemed terribly intimate.

Gripped by a turbulent complex of emotions, Matt stopped in midstride. He watched as Jay hefted Paige's suitcase and draped his free arm about her shoulders. He saw the way Paige smiled at Jay; that brave, winsome smile that brought the sunshine to her eyes. He watched as they turned and walked away, and when he saw how perfectly their steps matched, his mouth twisted into a rueful smile.

Obviously this was one auld acquaintance that was best forgotten.

He waited until Paige and Jay had moved out of sight before he collected his own luggage and left the terminal building.

As he hailed a taxi, Matt thought wearily that this was a hell of a way to start the new year. Seeing Paige again, being reminded that he couldn't have her, was enough to make him wish he *could* believe in good-byes.

Chapter One

April 8

"Hello, Irish."

Two short words, spoken in a voice from the past. A deep, compellingly masculine voice. A warm, uniquely seductive voice, as richly textured as velvet.

Paige Cavanaugh's hands were suddenly slippery with perspiration. Her grip on the telephone receiver tightened until her nails bit into her palm and the fine bones of her knuckles were a stark white beneath the ivory fairness of her skin.

Her legs gave way beneath her and as she sank into a chair she stared into the dressing-table mirror, watching the color drain from her face, watching her eyes darken from their usual sunny aquamarine to a stormy jade green.

When Paige saw that her eyes reflected her inner turmoil as surely as a bank of clouds massing over the ocean indicated a storm at sea, she quickly looked away from the mirror and focused on the painting that hung above the bed on the opposite wall.

Executed in an assembly-line style she thought of as motel-contemporary, it was the kind of painting motel chains bought by the gross to coordinate with the color schemes of their rooms, but she concentrated on the seascape as if it were a masterpiece, as if she must commit to memory the improbable whorls of avocado and beige acrylic.

Paige would have known that the voice on the telephone belonged to Matthew Jonas even if it hadn't been unique, even if she hadn't been waiting so anxiously for him to call. He was the only one who had ever called her "Irish."

The sound of Matt Jonas's voice was the first thing about him that she'd fallen in love with, but until this moment, Paige hadn't stopped to consider the impact that hearing his voice had always had upon her. She'd been too preoccupied with her plans, too busy rehearsing what she could say to Matt that might convince him to help her carry out those plans.

"Irish? Are you still there?" Matt's voice, sharp with concern—or was it impatience?—put an end to Paige's introspection.

"Y-yes, Matt," she answered shakily. "It's kind of you to return my call so promptly."

"I have to admit I'm curious as to why you'd want to contact me after—"

Don't be an ass! the skeptic in Matt cautioned, and he caught himself before he'd said anything too revealing. Why give Paige the satisfaction of knowing he'd kept track of the time since they'd parted?

"My God!" he went on warily. "How long has it been?"

Liar, his conscience chided.

Hang in there, Jonas! the skeptic approved. *With any luck at all, she won't have noticed you almost blew it.*

It became apparent Paige hadn't attached any significance to his hesitation when she replied, "It's been about eight years."

If she'd wanted to be totally precise, Paige could have told Matt it had been eight years, two months, three days, five hours, and some odd minutes. If she'd wanted to be completely honest, she would have told him it seemed like a lifetime. But just now, all she seemed to be capable of was a lame attempt to counteract her flat statement of fact.

"Do you mean to say you haven't been counting the days?" she added lightly.

Matt chose to ignore her question. "Judy, my secretary, said you sounded desperate."

"No!"

In the heavy silence that followed her protest, Paige envisioned Matt's face. His deepset eyes would be intent, his eyebrows drawn as he frowned, puzzling over the unwarranted vehemence of her denial.

She inhaled deeply and continued more calmly, "That is, I was *anxious* to talk to you, of course. That's why I phoned your office. But I'm hardly desperate." She punctuated her explanation with a brittle little laugh, hoping that Matt would be deceived into interpreting it as carefree.

"In that case, why not get to the point and tell me why you were trying to reach me," he suggested crisply, making it obvious that he'd seen through her poor efforts at subterfuge.

"Actually, I'd like to consult you—er, profession-ally. But it's about a personal matter of some urgency. I'd rather not discuss it on the phone." She paused, giving Matt the opportunity to comment, hoping he would offer to see her at his office and set the time for an appointment. When he didn't, she inquired hesi-tantly, "Could—would it be possible for us to meet?"

"Where are you staying?"

"At the Dunes Motel. It's just south of town, a block or so off Cabrillo Boulevard—"

"I know the place." Matt sounded brusque and businesslike now. "Look, Irish, Judy may have men-tioned that I've been in Sacramento for the past week, so there are a few things I have to square away here before I leave the office, but I could pick you up in a couple of hours. Say about nine o'clock? If you don't mind competing with a steak, we could go somewhere for dinner."

Although she felt too edgy to eat anything, Paige hurriedly accepted Matt's invitation. Her voice was steady as she gave him her room number, but after he'd broken the connection she remained unmoving, not even cradling the receiver until a series of elec-tronic beeps prompted her to replace it.

Her knees still felt too rubbery to support her, but she made herself get to her feet. She crossed to the luggage rack at the foot of the bed and opened her suitcase. Her clothes were crammed into it haphaz-ardly, another reminder of her uncharacteristic be-havior lately.

Ever since the day a month before when she'd found the newspaper clipping among her Aunt Rachel's papers, she had been lost in a limbo between wishful thinking and shattered dreams. Her moods were erratic, wavering swiftly from euphoria to despair. One minute her outlook was pessimistic, the next so optimistic that she'd found it hard to think about anything but the miraculous possibility the clipping had brought to light.

When she'd found no other clues among her aunt's things, she had tried to get in touch with an old family friend, Stella Ackerman, thinking that Stella would be able to confirm or deny her suspicions. But it had been more than seven years since Paige had seen her, and when she'd discovered that Stella no longer lived in Tuolumne County, she'd had to admit she was at an impasse.

Paige had considered conducting a search on her own, but she hadn't the faintest idea how to go about it—at least not in the thorough way she knew it must be done. If her suspicions had any foundation in fact, she must leave no stone unturned.

She'd thought about hiring a private investigator, but she had no way of paying his fee, and because the matter was so confidential, she hadn't felt there was anyone else she could turn to.

Then, in last Sunday's *Examiner,* there had been an article about the alarming increase of industrial espionage in one of California's better known aerospace firms. The exposé had run under Matt's by-line, along with an announcement that Matthew Jonas's column was to be a regular feature of the newspaper.

Paige hadn't heard from Matt Jonas since he'd been assigned to the capital of one of the more contentious Balkan countries. Sometimes, when the temptation became too great to withstand, she had permitted herself to be swept away on the waves of memory and she'd thought about him. There had been a number of times when she'd thought she'd actually seen him. As recently as last January, when she'd come through the San Francisco Airport on her way home from her Aunt Rachel's funeral, she had thought she'd caught a glimpse of Matt, but she'd lost track of him years ago.

He had always been a globe-trotter. He'd told her once that he'd developed his wanderlust as a little boy, when he'd noticed how different countries were depicted with different colors on the maps in the geography texts. He'd said that from that time it had been his ambition to travel until he'd found a country that deserved the color it was assigned.

Paige had wondered idly if he had fulfilled his ambition. But whether he had or not, it was surprising to hear that he was prepared to exchange his life in the fast lane, even for the prestige of a syndicated column.

It seemed heaven-sent that he had. Surely the same techniques must be involved whether they were applied to investigative journalism or to identifying which newspaper in California had printed a given article.

With nothing more than that slim hope to go on, on Monday morning Paige had notified her clients that she would be leaving town at the end of the week. She had advised them she might be away as long as a month, and she'd recommended another window design firm as a substitute until she returned.

After a humble beginning decorating the windows in the boutique where she'd worked as a salesclerk, she had built up her clientele by word-of-mouth—slowly, carefully, almost lovingly. Over the last five years, she had given her business the lavish attention she would have given her family, had she had one.

Until a few weeks ago, Paige wouldn't have believed that she would abandon her clients on such short notice. If anyone had told her that she would turn her back and walk away from the firm she had worked so hard to establish, she would have thought they were insane.

Yet she had done just that without a qualm, without even caring whether her clients would return to the fold when her search was over.

She had done it because she'd had no other choice. Because she was haunted by the clipping.

The idea that her aunt might have *lied,* the possibility that the baby hadn't been stillborn, that somewhere her child—Matt's child—might be *alive,* had become an obsession.

Chapter Two

Just when she needed to keep all her wits about her, the sound of Matt's voice had unlocked the floodgates of the past.

Her intentions to unpack forgotten, Paige lay down on the bed. She stared at the seascape without really seeing it as she fought to suppress the memories that filtered to the surface of her mind; memories that beguiled her with their brightness....

She'd met Matt Jonas a little more than eight and a half years before, when she was a student at Stanford. Although it had been her junior year, it was her first semester away from home, and she'd been pathetically eager to try her wings. She'd had two major goals that semester, neither of which had anything to do with acquiring a college education. The first was to make friends, and the second was to assert her independence.

She might have been the most naive college junior in the recent history of Stanford, but it hadn't taken her long to recognize that her clothes were no asset in her efforts to achieve her first goal. The dowdy skirts, starchy blouses, and prim sweater-sets her Aunt Ra-

chel insisted upon were all wrong. They set her apart,
creating a distance that was well-nigh impassable between herself and the other women in her dormitory.

Since conforming to the prevailing dress code
seemed a small price to pay for friendship, within a
week of her enrollment, Paige had found some blue
jeans and T-shirts in a secondhand store near the campus. In a way, her meeting with Matt had arisen directly from her innocent wish to blend into the crowd,
because after that, the wardrobe her aunt had provided was relegated to the back of the closet.

Even when she received an invitation to a Sunday
afternoon tea at Professor Jonas's home, she simply
cleaned her sneakers and donned faded jeans and a
T-shirt with the slogan "God is alive and failing English 101" emblazoned across the front.

It was not until she arrived at the professor's house
that it occurred to her Dr. Jonas might be offended by
the slogan, and only when it was too late did she learn
that it was customary for the students to dress more
formally for such an event.

Out of respect for the dignity of the occasion, the
other coeds were elaborately groomed, wearing bright
flowery dresses, and once again Paige was made conspicuous by her inappropriate attire.

Mrs. Jonas was gracious and tried to put Paige at
ease, but Dr. Jonas was cold and disapproving, especially when Paige had the temerity to disagree with
him about a poem.

She happened to be on the fringe of a group of students surrounding the professor when he quoted
some lines composed by a Housemaid Poet:

"O Moon, when I gaze on thy beautiful face,
Careering along through the boundaries of space,
The thought has often come into my mind
If I ever shall see thy glorious behind."

When Dr. Jonas finished reciting, as if on cue, the students snickered. He looked around the circle expectantly, and when the laughter had died down, he said, "Now, of what would you say those unfortunate lines are an example?"

"Bad poetry?" someone quipped, and everyone laughed again.

"Certainly that." The professor smiled benignly at the young man responsible for the joke. "Indeed, the lines are bad enough that it's my opinion they have no redeeming qualities whatsoever. Could you be more specific, however?"

When the young man didn't answer, Dr. Jonas scanned the group. "Anyone?" he invited, and that was when Paige spoke up.

"I know it's bad poetry," she said, "but I'm not sure I agree that it has nothing to redeem it. I think the poet's feelings are clear. It seems to me the lines convey a sense of her yearning."

With a frosty smile at Paige, Dr. Jonas replied, "My dear Miss Cavanaugh, a scream conveys feelings too, but that does not mean it's poetry."

After that, the few women Paige knew at the tea were embarrassed to be seen with her, and she found herself an outcast.

Regretting her brashness, she stood on the sidelines, nursing a cup of punch until the time came when she could slip away from the gathering without attracting further attention. But the longer she waited, the more crowded the room became, and the less likely it seemed she would be able to make an unobtrusive exit.

Every bit of floor space between the spot where she was standing and the front door was occupied. Any area not taken up by one or another of Dr. Jonas's guests was filled with heavy, dark, intricately carved furniture that reminded Paige of the old-fashioned living room suite in Aunt Rachel's parlor back home. The couch nearest her was upholstered in the same rusty-black damask as the one at home, and this added to the illusion of familiarity and increased her sensation of being imprisoned.

All at once, the walls seemed to close in on her and, feeling claustrophobic, she began working her way toward the hall. Perhaps she would find it easier to make her escape by the back door.

Paige had almost reached the end of the hall, checking each room she passed for a door leading outside, when she found a very different sort of room; one that was uncluttered and modern and cheerful despite the long shadows of twilight which were invading it.

Standing indecisively in the hallway, she surveyed the area. From the workmanlike desk in one corner and the bookshelves lining the walls, she concluded that she had stumbled upon the professor's sanctum sanctorum. Then she saw the glass doors standing open to the back terrace, and she forgot about discretion and hurried toward them.

The indirect lighting was at a low setting, and because the lamps had not yet been turned on against the encroaching darkness, Paige had reached the French doors and paused for one last look at the study before she noticed the lustrous vases on the mantel. They appeared to be authentic celadon, and surely that was a Ming bowl in a place of honor on one of the bookshelves. But could the beautiful little figurine that graced the corner nearest the windows possibly be genuine?

"She's a Ming dynasty *Kuan Yin*," announced a resonant baritone voice behind her.

The sound of the voice seemed to embrace her, bringing with it a premonition that this man was going to be terribly important to her. The feeling was so intense that the skin on her forearms broke out in gooseflesh. Then, at the touch of a wall switch, the lamps came on and the premonition was gone.

Now that she had a clearer view of the statue, Paige stared at it, entranced. "She's lovely," she said in awed tones.

"Yes, she is," the vibrant, soft-spoken voice agreed.

"I've never seen such a statue outside of a museum." Paige hesitated briefly, then added, "Come to think of it, I've never seen one in a museum either—just in photographs."

Only as she finished speaking did she turn to face the man who had entered the study, and her heart accelerated to a sharp staccato when she saw that his appearance was as charismatic as his voice.

He was tall and rangy—almost thin really—and rather pale, but he was ruggedly attractive all the same. She was oddly pleased that his looks measured up to the promise of his voice.

He's Lincolnesque, Paige told herself. *Lincolnesque and sexy.*

He was wearing dark corduroy pants with a fishermen's knit sweater, and from the way the sweater fit, hanging loosely from his broad shoulders, she wondered if he'd lost a good deal of weight recently. Perhaps he had been ill.

At any rate, from the way he was dressed, she didn't think he was one of Dr. Jonas's guests. It was possible he was and that he was as uninformed about the dress code as she, but somehow Paige doubted that.

Whoever the man was, he'd stationed himself just inside the entry to the study. His hands were on his hips and he was observing her with hooded eyes, plainly demonstrating that he was not at all pleased to have found her there. Because he looked so arrogant and sounded so authoritative, she finally decided that he must be a member of the professor's family.

"The door was open," she offered defensively. "I was only looking for a way outside."

When the man limited his response to a negligent shrug, in an effort to overcome her tension, Paige nodded nervously toward the *Kuan Yin* and asked, "How do you happen to have her?"

"My grandfather was a medical missionary to China, as were his parents before him. He was born and raised there, and until he and my grandmother had to return to the States when the war broke out in the 1930s, he'd been in this country only to attend college and medical school here at Stanford. When he and my grandmother were forced to come back to California permanently, they salvaged what they could from their home in China. Mostly they brought smaller objects that had been in the family for a long time—things they prized for their sentimental value.

"The *Kuan Yin* was considered indispensable because, after many years of longing for a child, my grandmother followed the custom of the Chinese and prayed to her for deliverance from her barren state. Granddad, strict Methodist that he was, was horrified until it became apparent that her prayers had been granted. My mother was born exactly nine months later, and that made a believer out of him.

"I guess you could say that was the start of a family tradition, since my mother swears that she also threw herself on the mercy of *Kuan Yin* before she succeeded in becoming pregnant."

Her eyes shining with appreciation of the story, Paige glanced at the man, but her smile faded when he didn't return it. Although his explanation had been easily given and his tone was friendly, he hadn't moved from the doorway, and his watchful stance seemed hostile.

"I'm Matt Jonas, by the way," he said. "And you must be Paige Cavanaugh."

Dry-mouthed, Paige nodded. "How did you know my name?"

"Doc's mentioned you."

She had to stifle the urge to giggle at the way Matt had referred to his father. It was unthinkable to her that anyone would have the nerve to call the graying, scholarly, eminently distinguished professor of English by a nickname. She marveled that even someone as closely related to him as his son was courageous enough to do so.

The impulse to laugh died when Matt ran his fingers through his hair and she was struck by the shakiness of the gesture.

"Are you all right?" she inquired.

"I'm okay." With a wry grimace, he disclosed, "I just finished a round of golf, and I guess I should have called it quits after the front nine."

As he replied, Matt moved away from the door. He walked toward her, not stopping until he'd reached her side. His mouth was stern, but his dark eyes were smiling as they traveled over her delicately modeled features.

For a few seconds his eyes rested on the generous curve of her mouth and the determined little chin that was softened by a dimple. Finally his gaze settled on her luxuriant mane of chestnut-colored hair.

If there was one thing about her appearance that Paige was sinfully proud of, it was her hair. On that day, she had brushed it away from her face and caught it at the crown of her head with a barrette so that the long tresses trailed down her back in a silky skein that seemed too heavy for the fragile stem of her neck to support.

Acting on a whim, Matt gave her ponytail a playful

tug, and when she raised her startled gaze to his, he grinned.

"Doc described you very well. He said you had fiery hair, a milk-and-roses complexion, eyes like sunlight on tropical seas, and that you're the embodiment of an Irish colleen. He also said you might decide you'd like me to tutor you for your Medieval Lit. class."

Not for a moment did Paige believe that Dr. Jonas had described her in such flattering terms. He had recommended she arrange to be tutored, and he must have given his son a factual description of her, but she was certain that the lyrical embellishments were Matt's own. She was also unaccustomed to personal compliments. Her cheeks burned with a color as fiery as the red highlights in her hair as she admitted, "I have been having trouble keeping up with your father's class."

"Well then, Irish, how about it? I'm on sick leave from my job to recuperate from an accident, so I'm going to be stuck in Palo Alto for the rest of the semester. And Medieval Lit. is one of my strongest subjects. Doc would have drummed me out of the family years ago if it weren't. It's been his favorite topic of dinner-table conversation for as long as I can remember."

"I—I don't know. That is, I'm not sure—"

"I can see you have your doubts," Matt inserted dryly, "but can't you state them a bit more clearly?"

Paige sighed. "It's only that I wouldn't feel right about taking up so much of your time without paying you, and I don't have any extra money."

"Don't be silly," Matt said dismissively. "You'd be doing me a favor, giving me something to do to pass the time till I have medical clearance to go back to work."

"Even so—"

"Okay, then, how about this? I'll teach you Medieval Lit and you can teach me something else. What's your best subject?"

Taking Matt's suggestion seriously, Paige thought this over for a moment before she replied, "Biology, I suppose. That's what got me my scholarship. But I don't think there's much I could teach you about the birds and the bees."

Matt nodded solemnly, but she saw amusement lurking in his eyes. "From the looks of you, I'd say that's a valid assumption. But all is not lost. There must be something else—" He glanced suggestively at the boldly lettered slogan on her T-shirt and smiled before he went on. "Tell you what—I'll begin tutoring you, and in return you can promise to try and think of something to teach me. I've got a hunch you're more versatile than you give yourself credit for."

Once again his eyes strayed over her, and this time he seemed to stare for an awfully long time at the tender outline of her mouth and at her gently rounded breasts.

"In fact," said Matt as if he were thinking out loud, "I'll bet you have more than your share of hidden talents. And even if you don't, I think I might enjoy tutoring a young lady who's a philosopher as well as a scholar and a rebel."

His grin slowly broadened, and in that instant, Paige knew that she was utterly lost. Whatever Matthew Jonas asked of her, if it was within her power to give it to him, she would.

Chapter Three

The day after Professor Jonas's tea, Paige made a number of inquiries about Matthew Jonas. She learned that he worked as a correspondent for United Press International, and that the accident he'd mentioned so casually had not been an accident at all. He'd been wounded while reporting on an attempted coup in one of the emerging African nations.

Her neighbors in the dorm knew Matt only by reputation, but they were more than willing to answer her questions. One of the graduate students, a willowy redhead named Maida Ormond, was intrigued by Paige's interest in Matt.

"Incredible!" Maida exclaimed, rolling her eyes dramatically. "You believe in starting at the top, don't you?"

"Why do you say that?" asked Paige.

"Because it's obvious you've led a sheltered life, my child. And it's also obvious you're infatuated with Matt Jonas."

"What if I am? Is that so terrible?"

Maida shook her head. "Not if you don't expect him to fall for you."

"I don't," Paige replied evenly. "Do you think I don't know that Matt would never have given me a nickname like 'Irish' if he saw me as a potential sweetheart? If he were at all attracted to me, he'd have called me Paige, or he might have given me a pet name like Angel or Kitten or Princess—"

"You've been watching too many soap operas, but I can't quibble with your reasoning," said Maida. "So okay. It's your funeral. What do you wanna know about the guy?"

"Whatever you can tell me," said Paige.

"You understand I don't know him personally," Maida cautioned.

"Yes, yes, I understand."

"All right, then. From what I've heard about him, Matt Jonas could give Casanova a run for his money. I've heard tell that when he dies he wants his epitaph to read: 'So many women; so little time.' He plays the field, strictly by his own rules, and those who are— quote—in a position to know, claim that he's in a league by himself; a genuine, world-class heart-breaker."

Paige nodded. "Yes," she said, half to herself. "I thought he might be."

"But you're not discouraged?"

"No, I'm not."

"You should be," Maida said firmly. "You're sup-posed to be some kind of whiz-kid, Paige. You seem sensible enough in other respects. Can't you see that getting involved with a man like Matt Jonas is like playing with fire? Sooner or later, you're going to get burned.''

"He's only going to tutor me, Maida. I'm not thinking of going to bed with him or anything like that."

"Yeah, that's what they all say."

"It's the truth," said Paige.

"Probably it is," Maida acceded. "But I still say you're going to get burned."

Blithely ignoring Maida's warning, Paige telephoned Matt. They made arrangements to meet several afternoons a week, and for a while it seemed that Maida was wrong. Matt treated Paige as indulgently as if she were his not-too-clever kid sister.

His mother's attitude toward her was as warmly affectionate as Matt's. When their tutoring sessions ran overtime, she even insisted Paige join the family for dinner, and before long Paige began to look upon Eve Jonas as the mother she had never known.

Dr. Jonas remained aloof, but since he was that way with everyone but his wife, Paige hadn't taken his coldness personally.

The few months of that fall school term were the happiest time of her life. Her love for Matt burned so bright and clear that the world seemed brand-new. After studying with him, she could watch him leave to pick up his date of the evening without suffering the tiniest pang of jealousy, but that was partially because he went from one girl to the next so rapidly, she knew they were even more temporary in his life than she was.

Matt's mother took a dim view of his philandering.

Since he was twenty-seven, she thought it was time he started thinking seriously about marriage. She was also worried about him because he was supposed to be convalescing.

"I do wish you'd settle down, Matt," Eve Jonas chided him gently on one of the rare evenings that he was home for dinner. "That girl you introduced me to last week—Jacqueline, wasn't it? Now she impressed me as a very lovely young woman who'd have a lot to offer any man. I don't know why you can't be satisfied to see more of her and forget about going on to the next one."

Matt hid his irritation well, but Paige saw that his hand had clenched around his wineglass.

"This is quite an about-face," he replied lightly. "I can recall a time when you were violently opposed to my getting married."

"But you were only twenty then, Matt! Naturally I was concerned that you were too young, and I always knew that Carole wasn't ready for marriage."

Matt raised an eyebrow at his mother. "That's putting it mildly," he said sardonically. "In fact, that's about the nicest thing I've ever heard you say about Carole."

"Can you blame me? Really, Matthew, you hadn't been gone for a week when she started going out with other men."

"I know, Ma, I know. But she taught me a valuable lesson. Now I see a variety of girls for the same reason you don't serve meat loaf night after night after night."

Matt speared a bite of roast lamb with his fork and

turned the tines of the fork toward the ceiling, offering the chunk of lamb as a sort of visual aid before he
popped it into his mouth. He chewed with obvious
relish, and when he'd swallowed the lamb he said,
"What I mean is, life is a smorgasbord. You have
your choice of lamb or steak, prime ribs or spare ribs
or Southern-fried chicken. And when you've had
your fill of them, there's abalone and shrimp and
lobster, not to mention all the more exotic delicacies
that are just waiting to be sampled. So why should I be
willing to settle for a steady diet of hamburger?"

"You're wrong, Matt." Though she tried to look
reproachful, Eve Jonas couldn't keep from smiling.
"Life is not a perpetual smorgasbord, but even if it
were, gluttons have been known to wind up with a
jaded palate and a frightful case of indigestion. Besides, there must be a thousand and one ways of preparing hamburger."

"And your mother knows them all," said Professor
Jonas. He exchanged a long, loving glance with his
wife and added softly, "Scheherazade had nothing on
you, Eve."

While Paige had sensed a marked lack of warmth
between Matt and Dr. Jonas, the special brand of
closeness between Matt's parents was one of the
things that made her feel so privileged to have gained
admittance to the charmed circle of their lives.

Later that evening, she commented upon this to
Matt, saying, "I've never seen a couple as attuned to
one another as your mother and father. They seem
to be able to communicate without saying a word."

"So you've noticed how Doc goes all absentminded

in the middle of a sentence and forgets what he was about to say—"

"And your mother finishes it for him," Paige cut in, much to Matt's amusement.

Chuckling, he said, "My mother and Doc are so close, they're practically Siamese twins. If there is such a thing as soul mates, it's them. There have been times when I've felt shut out by their closeness. It's as if I'm an interloper who's on the outside, looking in."

"I know the feeling," Paige murmured.

"Yes, I imagine you do." Matt studied her thoughtfully. "That must be one of the biggest drawbacks to skipping grades in school the way you have. You've been able to keep up with the other students scholastically, but you can't skip stages of emotional and social development. In some ways, you've been left at the post. Even now it can't be easy for you, trying to find your niche among college juniors when you're only eighteen. Granted you've had a lot of practice—"

"Since I was six," she admitted dully, remembering how much it had hurt when her third-grade classmates had ignored her because she was "only a baby," while the first-graders shunned her because she was in the third grade. After a few weeks of that treatment, her Aunt Rachel hadn't had to cajole or threaten her nearly as much to get her to study. Books had become poor substitutes for friends, and she had learned to hide her hurt feelings beneath a veneer of cool indifference.

But now, with Matt, she let her guard down. It was only for a moment, but he saw how unhappy she was. In an effort to cheer her up, he ruffled her hair, grinned at her encouragingly, and said, "Maybe we can do something about it."

In the next few months, Matt did try to do something about her social life. He taught her about much more than medieval literature. He taught her the latest dance steps, and when he discovered she'd never learned to ride a bicycle, he taught her how to do that too.

His parents' home bordered the local country club, and on most weekdays they spent the early morning hours on the tennis courts while he tried to improve her backhand. She asked him to teach her golf, mostly because she was greedy for more time alone with him, and while they made their way around the course, he explained some of the more complicated social mores that had always been so mystifying to Paige. When, at long last, she began to make friends, he advised her on such diverse matters as clothes and boys and football games.

Only once did she balk at doing something Matt suggested. When Jay Lowndes, who was in the same chemistry lab as Paige, asked her to go to the Stanford-Cal game with him, a trace of her Aunt Rachel's rock-ribbed thriftiness surfaced, making Paige reluctant to accept the invitation.

"I don't know the first thing about football," she argued. "It seems to me it would be an awful waste of my time and Jay's money for me to go with him."

"And here I thought you were eager to try new things," Matt lamented. "Look, Irish, you don't have to understand football to enjoy yourself at the game. You'll go because you want to be with Jay, and who cares if you even watch what's happening down on the field. By halftime lots of the fans are so wiped out on martinis and Bloody Marys, they can't tell a punt from a hole in the ground anyway. A football game is a social event first and a sporting event second, and if you're a student at Stanford, the game with U.C. is where it's at.''

She hadn't wanted to disappoint Matt, so she'd gone to the game with Jay. She wore a white chrysanthemum in the lapel of her red plaid jacket, and she sat with Jay in the cheering section. She cheered till she was hoarse, stomped her feet and applauded until her feet and hands were numb, and drank hot-buttered rum from a thermos to chase away the cold. And although she had no idea which team won the game, she had a marvelous time.

When she had finished giving Matt a glowing report about her date, he asked, "Where did you go after the game?"

"Afterward? Why, to a party at someone's house."

"And after that?"

Wondering why Matt was pursuing the subject so doggedly, she replied slowly, "Jay took me home."

"Did he make a pass?"

"H-he kissed me that's all." She felt herself blushing as she added shyly, "He asked me to go to the beach at Santa Cruz with him next Saturday."

"Just the two of you?"

She shook her head. "There are several couples going."

"That's okay then," said Matt, as if she needed his permission.

"Honestly, Matt!" she protested. "I have had dates before, you know! I'm not a babe in the woods."

"Maybe not, but I'm not sure you'd recognize the big, bad wolf if he bit you on the behind, so your lesson for today is that there's safety in numbers."

"Is this another case of doing as you say and not as you do?" she complained tartly. "Or do you follow that rule too?"

"You'd better believe I follow it, Irish," Matt said dryly. "But in my case, it's not for quite the same reason."

Matt and she had been the best of friends for nearly three months when, in some subtle way, their relationship began to change. Paige had never been able to figure out why the change had started. Perhaps Matt had guessed that she was in love with him. Perhaps he was trying to let her down gently. Whatever the reason, suddenly it was as if Matt were purposely erecting barricades between them. Whenever the opportunity presented itself, he seemed to be sending out danger signals.

And she knew to the moment when she had become sexually aware of Matt. It was on the night before Thanksgiving, when she'd seen Matt and Carole at a cafe near the campus.

When Matt came into the restaurant that evening with a shapely blonde on his arm, Maida leaned across the table and whispered, "Don't look now, but your tutor just came in with his ex-fiancée."

Paige would have automatically turned toward the entrance, but Maida hissed, "I said don't look!"

Only a moment later, however, Matt and Carole passed by their booth. Matt stopped to say hello to Paige and he might have suggested they join Paige and Maida if Carole hadn't wandered to another table.

"Come on, darling," she called. "I'm famished, and I'm just dying for the café au lait you promised me."

Matt replied with a double entendre about her "insatiable appetite," but for all his teasing, he'd certainly seemed happy to be with her.

They'd chosen to sit at a booth no more than fifteen feet away, and Paige observed the older woman surreptitiously, thinking that it was easy to see why Matt found Carole attractive. Any man would. Her tawny hair and golden skin radiated vivacity, and she had more than her fair share of sex appeal.

Dressed as she was in her jeans and baggy sweater, Paige felt drab and uninteresting compared to Carole, who wore a bias-cut kelly-green dress that clung revealingly to the flawless curves of her body. It was apparent that she wasn't wearing a bra, and Paige couldn't help noticing Matt's admiring appraisal of Carole's well-displayed charms.

Even as Paige watched, Matt lifted Carole's hand to his lips and pressed possessive little kisses on each of her fingertips, in the palm, and then on her inner wrist.

"Lord have mercy," Maida whispered. "Did you see that move? That's what I call downright sexy."

"Yes, it was," Paige murmured.

It had been an oddly intimate gesture, especially

considering that Matt knew very well that she and Maida were watching. In fact, she felt like a voyeur, and she turned decisively away from Matt and Carole and promised herself that she would not look at them again. But Maida kept up a running commentary on their behavior.

"The waitress just brought their order," said Maida. "Matt's playing eye contact games with Carole, and she's eating very suggestively. It's so trite, it's enough to make you sick, but he seems to be enjoying it. Now she's fiddling with his shirt buttons, and—Oh, wow! She must really be hungry, because she's nibbling on his ear. I give them five minutes, tops, before they leave."

Paige wanted to scream at Maida to stop it. She wanted to clap her hands over her ears and shriek, "I don't want to hear this," but she drank her coffee and remained silent.

"What did I tell you?" Maida said, grinning smugly. "They're getting ready to leave. Matt's helping Carole into her jacket."

Despite her resolve not to, while Matt and Carole waited at the cash register to pay their bill, Paige glanced at them again. She saw the proprietary way Matt lifted Carole's hair outside the collar of her coat. Then he slipped his arm around her shoulders. In response, Carole snuggled closer to him. She tilted her piquant face toward his and smiled seductively, and when she rubbed her cheek against the back of his hand, Paige thought viciously, *They should have ordered a saucer of cream and forgotten the café au lait. She looks as if she's going to start purring any second.*

As soon as this thought had formed, Paige felt a stab of self-annoyance.

What's happening to me? she wondered. She was not usually prone to cattiness—

It's jealousy. The realization blazed into her consciousness. That, of course, was the answer. She was jealous of Càrole. Jealous because, while Matt had tweaked her ponytail and ruffled her curls, he'd never touched her hair the way he'd touched Carole's. Jealous because she wanted it to be her, Paige, flirting with Matt in the curve of his arm. Jealous because she wanted to rub her own cheek against the back of his lean, strong hand, and because she wanted Matt to want it to be her doing those things.

She was jealous because she wanted all that—and much, much more. But more than anything else, she was jealous because she would never have it.

To Matt she was just a child. She was good for a few laughs and a lot of ego-boosting unquestioning adoration—nothing more.

Despairingly, she told herself, *It will never be me. Can never be me.* She bent her head over her coffee cup and clenched her hands together in her lap until her fingers grew bloodlessly numb. She was riveted by the strength of her emotions, and she didn't actually see Matt and Carole leave the café, but she heard Maida's final tormenting remark.

"What do you think, Paige? This must be the first case on record where caffeine's been used as a sexual stimulant," Maida said, laughing at her own witticism.

Chapter Four

It was strange, thought Paige, how one event led to another seemingly unrelated event, and that one to another, and that one to the next as inevitably as a row of dominoes toppling.

If Matt hadn't been wounded, if she hadn't been awarded a scholarship that paid most of her expenses at Stanford, they might never have met. And if she hadn't fallen asleep after her chemistry final and missed the afternoon bus to Alder Creek, they might never have become lovers.

But she and Matt had met, and she had overslept on that fateful day.

Eight years ago, she thought numbly. A little more than that now. But because hearing Matt's voice had added to her memories the same intensity of emotion she'd had then, it might almost have happened yesterday....

It was the week before Christmas, but the coming holiday seemed relatively insignificant because it was finals week at Stanford. By Friday evening, when

Paige had taken her last exam, she was punch drunk from too much studying, too few regular meals, and too little sleep.

She had also missed her bus home, which meant she'd have to talk the student housing office into letting her stay in the dorm an extra night. Thank goodness Aunt Rachel had been understanding when she'd called to tell her that, after staying up all night cramming for her chemistry final, she'd made the mistake of having a catnap, and she'd slept right through her alarm.

In a way Paige hated to see the term end because it meant Matt wouldn't be tutoring her, but since he no longer seemed to be concerned that her feelings for him would cause her to become a pest, she was positive she would see him fairly often just the same.

Hadn't he asked her to keep him company this evening? "Since the folks are away at Tahoe," he'd said, "your aunt's loss can be my gain."

Paige was running as she crossed the nearly deserted campus in the direction of the Jonas house. The evening was blustery and an icy rain was falling. The combination of cold and damp was so penetrating that she felt the chill of it to her bones, but the weather didn't dampen her spirits.

When they'd talked on the phone, Matt had sounded as if he were in good spirits too, but Paige had sensed that he was discouraged, and she was determined to cheer him up.

Only yesterday his doctor had told him it would be a minimum of another two months before he'd be well enough to go back to work.

"Dr. Forrest said if all I had to do was sit in an office, or if my assignments took me only to places where medical facilities are readily available, I'd be well enough now," Matt had reported.

But Matt's working conditions were not so predictably civilized. At times they could be very uncivilized indeed, which was how he'd been injured in the first place.

Matt had been disheartened when he'd heard the doctor's verdict, but Paige's Christmas present to him had offered a temporary distraction. She'd made him a sampler, into which she had carefully cross-stitched the motto, "Warning: The Surgeon General Has Determined That Brushfire Wars Are Hazardous To Your Health."

When he'd opened it, Matt had laughed heartily. Then he'd said, "I'm touched, Irish, that you spent so much time on my gift when you have so little time to spare." As if to offer her an extra incentive, he'd added, "If you've done as well as I expect you have on your Medieval Lit final, maybe I'll let you see my scar."

"Is that a threat or a promise?" she'd asked doubtfully.

"Cute," Matt retorted. "Not funny. Not original. But cute. I'll thank you to have some respect for your elders."

He'd pretended to take offense, thinking that she was teasing, but she really did have mixed emotions about seeing the scar. She wasn't sure she wanted to see the evidence of how dangerously close Matt had come to dying from the wound.

As she dodged a bicycle rider on that rainy December night, Paige reminded herself that Matt was very much alive. In some ways he was the most alive person she'd ever known. The mere prospect of being with him was enough to make her happy, but besides that she was in a mood to celebrate because she'd made it through the tough competition of her first semester at Stanford.

She felt so lighthearted that she told herself, *You, Paige Cavanaugh, are the luckiest woman in the world.* And in that moment, she honestly believed it.

She was even looking forward to going home for the semester break. She was confident she'd done well in her classes, and if Aunt Rachel was satisfied with her grades, maybe she wouldn't constantly pressure her to use her vacation wisely. Maybe she wouldn't insist that every waking minute of her niece's day be filled with books and studies. Maybe they could just relax and have a pleasant Christmas together.

Paige was still running when she turned into the Jonas's drive, but halfway to the house she had to slow to a walk. The house was dark and the front yard was deeply shadowed. The windows of Matt's studio apartment above the garage were brightly lighted though. She started to run again when the garage came into view, but she'd taken only a few steps when she collided with Matt.

"Whoa, there." His hands settled on her shoulders to steady her. "Where's the fire?"

"Matt!" she gasped. "You startled me, suddenly appearing out of nowhere like that."

"Well, excuse me," Matt countered, chuckling. "I

might point out, though, that all I did was walk down my own stairs. Anyway, I thought we'd agreed that I'd drive by your dorm and give you a ride tonight.''

They had, but she hadn't wanted to wait any longer to see him. "I—er, I felt like taking a stroll,'' she extemporized.

"Sure you did, and why not?'' Matt tipped his head back and caught some raindrops in his mouth before he said facetiously, "Lovely weather we're having this evening, isn't it.''

He started up the stairs toward his apartment, and feeling rather chastened, Paige followed close behind him. When he reached the landing at the top of the stairs, he opened the door and stood aside to allow her to precede him.

"Where's your umbrella?'' he asked.

"I lost it last week.''

"And you haven't gotten round to replacing it?''

"Not yet.''

Matt frowned. "There are times, Irish, when I think you need a keeper.''

"There are times,'' she replied, "when I think you do too.''

While he had been hanging her slicker and his own Windbreaker away in the guest closet, she had anxiously scanned his face, and she was alarmed by how haggard he looked.

"Did you sleep at all last night?'' she asked.

"Some.'' He closed the closet door and leaned against it wearily. "Mostly I paced the floor and tried to think of some way of getting Dr. Forrest to change his mind.''

"Did it ever occur to you that you should follow his orders?"

"All he says is take it easy and have patience. *Patience!*" Matt repeated abrasively. "How's that for being useless when what I really want is to get back to work!"

"But there's nothing else you can do, Matt."

"I know that, Irish, and that's the hell of it! Frankly, I don't know how much longer I'll be able to put up with Mom riding her hobbyhorse about my settling down and providing her with grandchildren."

He looked so miserable, it seemed only natural to try to console him, and when Paige put her arm around his waist, he wrapped his arms around her shoulders and hugged her close.

"I'm sorry, Matt, but it's just that she's worried about you. After all, you were critically injured, and you don't take very good care of yourself. You forget to eat properly, and you don't get nearly enough rest."

"Ah, but there's a method to my madness, Irish. Women take one look at me and they can't resist trying to mother me."

"But not for long."

Matt pressed his cheek against her hair. "Now how would a sheltered little girl like you know a thing like that?"

"I may seem like a little girl to you, but I'm a woman, Matt. I know it the same way any other woman would." Matt stiffened with surprise at her response, but Paige went on recklessly, "I don't think you should stay here alone, especially with Christmas coming up. Maybe you should join your parents at Tahoe after all. That might take your mind off things—"

"No!"

Puzzled by Matt's abruptness, Paige pulled away from him enough to see his face. His expression was rigidly controlled, very nearly masklike, and his eyes were opaque and inscrutable.

"Let's just change the subject," he said harshly, setting her roughly away from him. "Now where would you like to have dinner?"

"I'm not really dressed to go out anywhere." She glanced disparagingly at her jeans and T-shirt. "Could we eat here?"

"If you'd rather."

"I'll fix something then. What would you like?"

Matt shrugged. "There's not much to choose from. The cupboards are almost bare."

Paige peered into the refrigerator. "There are eggs, though, and some cheese. How about an omelet?"

Matt didn't reply. He pulled out a chair and slouched into it, sitting hunched over the table with his head propped in his hands.

Taking his lack of response to mean he had no objections to her proposal, Paige went to work in the kitchenette. After some searching, she found a suitable frying pan, a mixing bowl, a whisk, and the other utensils she would need. She began preparing the omelet, adding seasoning and herbs to the eggs and whipping the mixture until it was light and frothy.

She had grated a wedge of cheese and was slicing bread for toast when, without preamble, Matt declared, "Doc's not my father."

.Paige was dismayed by the unexpected statement. Her dexterous motions stopped, and she spun around to stare at Matt incredulously.

"Oh, he's my father legally," said Matt without inflection, "but my mother was married before—to Doc's older brother. Doc adopted me after he and Mom were married, and Lord knows he's tried, but I don't think he's ever stopped resenting me. After all these years, he's still threatened by his older brother—and, I suppose, by me. It's senseless, but apparently that's the way he feels."

The discovery that a man of Dr. Jonas's caliber could be jealous of his stepson was shocking to Paige. Naturally she had noticed the professor's possessiveness with Matt's mother, but she'd assumed it was simply another manifestation of their closeness.

She wanted to denounce the injustice of his treatment of Matt, and she knew she should make some response to Matt's disclosure, but she couldn't force the words past the lump in her throat.

Matt didn't notice her lapse, however. He seemed to be lost in thought, and after a momentary silence, he went on abstractedly, "The strange thing is, when my mother told me she and Doc were going to get married, I was overjoyed. I thought we'd be a real family. I thought I was finally going to have a dad, just like all the other guys did. But it never happened. Probably I was overeager. I know I came on much too strong with Doc."

"How—" Paige cleared her throat. "How do you mean?"

"Well, Doc was in his late thirties when he and my

mother were married, and he was very set in his ways. Granddad used to say that Doc was a born zealot because he was convinced the only right way to do anything was his way, and I suppose I didn't give him enough time to make the adjustment to having a rambunctious seven-year-old on his hands.''

Frowning reflectively, Matt qualified, ''Don't think I didn't give it my best shot, because I did. We both did. But even when I gave it my best, I wasn't exactly a model of good behavior, and I must have tried Doc's patience once too often. Eventually the situation between us deteriorated into a war of wills.''

''You must have been terribly disappointed, Matt. I can't tell you how sorry I am—''

''Don't waste your sympathy on me, Irish, because I don't deserve it. If you have to feel sorry for someone, pity my poor mother. She's the one who's been caught in the cross fire all these years.''

Although Paige disagreed with Matt, since he obviously wasn't the sort of man who would want anyone to feel sorry for him, she didn't pursue the issue. Slowly, as if her movements must be carefully synchronized, she began slicing another piece of bread.

''You said you were seven when your mother remarried?''

''That's right,'' Matt answered evenly.

''Then do you remember your—your real father?''

''Barely.''

Matt's reply was so terse, Paige was afraid she had offended him with her question. But after a brief hesitation, he went on. ''I saw very little of him, and he died when I was five. He was a journalist too, but his luck ran out on him and he was killed in a border skirmish in the Near East. My mother used to build him up. When I was a kid, she seemed to idolize him. She talked about him as if he were Errol Flynn and Albert Schweitzer rolled into one.

"Doc, on the other hand, tore him down. According to him, my father was nothing more than a legendary bum. But the message that came through, loud and clear, was that both of them see my father as being larger than life, so it's hard to distinguish fact from fiction. It's confusing now, but it was even more confusing when I was a youngster."

As she listened, Paige focused on the omelet, which was browning nicely in the pan. She buttered the toast when it popped up. Her back was toward Matt, but she was aware that he had gotten to his feet and removed a liquor bottle and some glasses from the cupboard by the breakfast bar.

"Here," Matt directed, sliding a glass with amber-colored liquid at the bottom of it along the counter in front of her. "Drink this."

She picked the glass up and sniffed it. "What is it?"

"Calvados," he said shortly. "Will you just drink it and try not to be so damned picky?"

She swallowed a little of the brandy, choking a bit over the fiery sensation it caused in her throat. Her eyes were still tearing when she divided the omelet and the toast. After transferring the warmed plates to the breakfast bar, she sat on the stool next to him.

Although Matt attacked his food ravenously, as if he hadn't eaten all day, Paige doubted he knew what he was eating. But his plate was nearly empty before he pushed it aside and poured another pony of brandy into his snifter. He swirled the heavy crystal a few times and drained it in a single swallow. Then, holding the snifter to one eye like a lens, he studied Paige through the empty glass before setting it down on the counter.

"Do you know, Irish," he remarked meditatively, "I don't think I've ever heard you mention any relatives except for your aunt."

"That's because Aunt Rachel is all the family I have. I don't know who my father was, and my mother disappeared when I was a baby. She left me with my aunt while she went to San Francisco for a few days, supposedly to look for a job, and she never came back for me."

Paige took a sip from her own glass before she went on, welcoming the sting of the brandy that gave her a ready excuse for the tears that were gathering at the backs of her eyes.

"It's been hard for Aunt Rachel, trying to live down the stigma of my illegitimacy in a town as insular as Alder Creek, but she's been good to me. She's very conscientious about providing whatever advantages she can. In fact, she's dutiful almost to a fault. There's been more than one time when she's gone without something because of me."

"And she's never let you forget for a minute how much you owe her," Matt surmised.

"No," said Paige. "Not consciously, anyway. She is demanding, but it's only because she has such high hopes for me."

"My experience has been just the opposite." Matt

smiled but there was no humor in it. "No matter how Doc tries, he can't bring himself to expect very much of me. He'd be the first to tell you that hanging is too good for me."

Paige stared at Matt, her eyes wide and troubled. Although his phrasing had been impersonal, he'd sounded as if he were warning her to keep her distance from him. And now he was watching her with a guarded intensity that increased her uneasiness. The little appetite she'd had suddenly deserted her. Wanting to escape Matt's scrutiny, she slid off the stool and began rinsing the dishes.

"Do you want to wash or dry?" she asked lightly, trying to ease the tension between them.

"I'll dry," Matt replied.

They worked together quietly, clearing away the dishes they'd used for their meal and the others that were stacked on the counter as well. Because the kitchenette was only a little larger than a closet, it was impossible to avoid bumping into one another as they worked. Every time Matt brushed against her, every time he had to reach around her to put something away in the cupboard on her side of the sink, Paige's awareness of him soared to a new level. Before half the dishes were washed, she was so self-conscious that she felt she was going to drop the plates and glasses.

When she did break one of the coffee mugs, Matt observed blandly, "I never noticed it before, Irish, but you're a real butterfingers. Take it easy, or I won't have any dishes left."

Of course, that only made Paige more nervous. She

was keenly aware of Matt's eyes on her as she waited for the sink to drain so she could scour it. She had already sprinkled in the cleanser when Matt's hand closed around her wrist. With his other hand, he took the can of cleanser and set it down on the counter.

"Leave it," he said peremptorily. His hands moved to her waist and he turned her around to face him. "You've done your good deed for the day. You've fed me dinner, cleaned my kitchen, listened to my tale of woe, and given me brandy and sympathy."

"It was your brandy," she replied breathlessly.

"So it was."

A smile tugged at the corners of his mouth as he cupped her face between his palms. All at once he was stroking her cheeks, smoothing the silky tendrils of hair away from her temples, tracing her features with his fingertips, looking at her as if he had never really seen her before.

"It's funny," he mused, "but I've told you things tonight that I've never told anyone else."

Paige couldn't tear her eyes away from the sensual curve of his mouth. *He's going to kiss me,* she thought. Her heart was racing, leaping like a wild thing against her breastbone. She was so giddy with wonder at the prospect of Matt's kissing her that she was afraid she might faint.

But Matt didn't kiss her. Instead, he stepped away from her and said, "It's time I drove you back to your dorm."

Paige leaned weakly against the counter at her back. "The semester's over," she replied in a subdued voice, looking at Matt with her love for him shining from her eyes. "I don't have to leave. I—I could stay here—with you."

For a few seconds, Matt's expression registered disbelief. If Paige hadn't honestly believed he shouldn't be alone, she would have been ashamed of herself for taking advantage of the situation at a time when his defenses were down.

Then his eyes left her face to roam over her body. His gaze lingered on her breasts, on the swell of her hips and the lissome taper of her thighs, and she fervently wished she were wearing a dress instead of blue jeans and an oversized T-shirt that were not at all flattering to her slight figure.

Was Matt disgusted by the brazen way she had offered herself to him? Was he secretly laughing at her childish attempt at seduction?

Oh, God! She couldn't bear that. She would rather have his contempt than have him regard her as some kind of bad joke.

His eyes were shuttered when they returned to her face. "Irish," he said softly, "If you have any sense at all, you'll *run,* not walk to the nearest exit."

"Is that what you want me to do, Matt?"

"No! Heaven help me, but no, it isn't." He reached out with one hand as if he wanted to touch her, but then he caught himself and groaned, "Damn! If only you weren't so young."

Paige laughed shakily. She desperately wished he would take her in his arms, that he would kiss her, but his hands were knotted into fists as if he were fighting for control.

"If I were to hurt you," he muttered, "I could

never forgive myself. If you stay, I'd like you to be very sure it's what you want to do. I have enough on my conscience without being guilty of seducing you."

"How could you be guilty of that?" she asked. "You're not giving me much encouragement."

"I'm trying my damnedest not to, Irish."

That grudging admission was all the encouragement she needed.

"I'm staying," she announced firmly.

Matt inclined his head. "Very well. Why don't you go ahead and take your turn in the bathroom while I make up the bed. You'll find a toothbrush in the medicine cabinet, and I believe there's even a robe in there you could use."

Matt turned away from her to stride toward the couch and, moving like an automaton, Paige carried out his instructions.

She went into the bathroom and closed the door quietly. She found the toothbrush, still neatly packaged in its clear plastic tube, and used it. She undressed and folded her clothes, but when she saw the monogram on the green satin robe that was hanging on a hook on the back of the door, she knew she could never wear it.

Still holding the robe, she sat on the edge of the tub and outlined the first initial of the monogram with her forefinger.

C stands for Carole, she thought, and for the clinical way Matt had dealt with her advances, and for the cruel comparison he'd forced her to make right now.

For a long time she sat there, with the cold enamel of the tub numbing the back of her thighs, hesitating because she knew why Matt had treated her so coolly. She knew why he'd brought the robe to her attention.

He'd thought seeing it would make her change her mind, but she wouldn't! She would show Matthew Jonas how wrong he was about her. She would prove to him she wasn't a child.

Paige squared her shoulders with determination and stood up. After carefully replacing the robe on its hook, she removed her T-shirt from the stack of clothing. As she pulled the shirt on, she was thankful it was oversized. It reached almost to midthigh, and while it wasn't a sexy green satin robe, neither was it unlike the shorty nightgowns worn by some of the women in the dorm. At least it would allow her some modesty while she ran the gauntlet from the bathroom to the living room.

When at last she let herself out of the bathroom, she deliberately left the door open, for she knew that the light spilling through at her back would silhouette her body, giving Matt a glimpse of the sweetly rounded curves that revealed the woman.

But Matt didn't look at her. He called out, "You've been in there so long, I was about to organize a search party."

He hadn't undressed, but he'd opened the sofa bed and was stretched out on it, reading an article in *Foreign Affairs* magazine. Except for the lamp on the table nearest him, the living room was dark, but when he finally lowered the magazine and looked at Paige, she saw his eyes widen with some indefinable emotion. She saw the agitated way his throat worked.

She was trembling, but her posture was proudly

erect as she walked toward him, and his expression of open admiration was ample reward for her daring.

"My God," he said hoarsely. "I thought you'd gotten cold feet—that you were trying to work up the courage to tell me you want to leave after all."

Paige was unable to keep the tremor from her voice as she replied, "I love you, Matthew Jonas, and I'm staying. But my feet *are* cold."

Matt's face was strangely solemn. The magazine slid to the floor and was forgotten as he held his hands out to her.

"Come here," he invited gravely. "I'll warm them for you."

Had she truly seen love in his eyes, or had she only imagined it? Real or imagined, it made no difference, because in a few more steps she had reached the sofa, and when she put her own hands confidingly into his, he pulled her down beside him and into the blissful warmth of his arms.

He held her gently at first, scattering soft kisses across her cheeks, her forehead, her chin, the corners of her mouth, almost as if he were afraid she might break.

Her fingers were shaking with eagerness as she tried to unbutton his shirt. When Matt stopped kissing her and raised his head to look at her inquiringly, she whispered, "I want to touch you."

He peeled the shirt off over his head without bothering to undo the rest of the buttons. Then he lay back against the pillows, smiled and said, "Be my guest."

She began by running her hands over his face, learning his features all over again with her fingertips, delighting in his well-marked brows and proud, straight nose, loving his craggy jaw and stubborn chin. His mouth was heaven. Her fingers trailed over his throat and neck, and by the time she arrived at his shoulders, she was drunk with the feel of him. She reveled in the ruggedness of his shoulders, in his smoothly muscled chest.

Then she found the scar and she followed it along his rib cage. It was frighteningly long, extending almost to his hip, then angling across his abdomen before it ended just below his navel.

Raising onto one elbow, Paige looked at the scar. Tears sprang into her eyes when she saw how the angry red of it marred the hard masculine beauty of Matt's torso. With infinite tenderness, she leaned over and touched her lips to the blemish. She heard the sharp intake of Matt's breath at the contact as she began tracking its jagged course with kisses, and in the next instant his hands had fastened in her hair and pulled her face close to his.

"Where did you learn that little trick?"

"Trick?" She shook her head helplessly, mystified by the question, startled by the wariness in his eyes. "I don't understand. Did I do something wrong?"

Matt laughed raggedly. "You really haven't a clue, have you, sweetheart?"

She could feel him trembling all over as his arms closed around her, sweeping her into a breathtaking embrace, pinning her beneath him when he turned her onto her back.

"Open your mouth," he demanded against her

lips, and when she did, he kissed her deeply, moving his mouth on hers as if he wanted to devour her. He was almost savage in his urgency until he realized he was hurting her.

The erotic play of his tongue continued. It intensified. But his hold on her gentled and he began caressing her tenderly. His hands skimmed over her, pausing to mold themselves to the small of her back, the hollow of her waist, the undercurve of her breasts, lingering when they found some new pleasure point, working their sorcery until her head was reeling and her flesh seemed to leap to his touch. Beneath his skilled persuasion, each individual cell of her body yearned for greater intimacies, and she abandoned herself to the mindless, glorious, riotous sensations he was evoking.

She felt bereft when Matt left her to pull off the rest of his clothes, but when he tried to remove her T-shirt, she stiffened and kept her arms close to her sides.

Now that the moment of truth was near, she felt uncertain and inadequate. She closed her eyes and turned her face away from his. She knew it was a childish thing to do, but because she felt so terribly vulnerable, she kept her eyes tightly shut in spite of his coaxing, as if by not being able to see herself, she might actually become invisible.

Matt tried teasing her. Referring to the miniscule line of lettering on the white cotton cloth that covered her breast, he said, "According to your T-shirt, you're ready and willing."

"It doesn't say that. It says—"

"What, Irish? What does it say?"

"It says, 'If you can read this, you're close enough to love me.'"

"The way it finishes is 'Love me, love me, love me,'" Matt corrected her, his voice husky. "In my book, that has the same connotation as ready and willing."

He cupped her breast with his hand, shaping its softness in the warm bowl of his palm, but she still resisted him, still kept her eyes closed and her arms rigid. She could feel herself blushing all over.

"If you're afraid, you don't have to go through with it," said Matt. "It's not too late to back out, you know."

"No!" she cried, and was even more embarrassed as she confessed, "Well, maybe I'm a little afraid, but all I'm afraid of is that you'll be disappointed."

"Never!"

When she didn't respond to this reassurance, Matt tried a slightly different approach. In the midst of nuzzling her ear, he whispered, "If you're offended by the sight of the human body, perhaps you should complain to the maker."

Her eyes flew open involuntarily, and when she saw that Matt was smiling lazily down at her, she giggled and tried to guess the source of his quote.

"Oscar Wilde?"

Matt shook his head. His face was so close to hers that they rubbed noses. "Close, but no cigar. Lenny Bruce."

After that, she was utterly pliant as he stripped off the T-shirt. For a heart-stopping time he only looked at her. Then he began running one hand over her, charting the gracefully rounded curves from breast to belly to hip.

His hand returned to caress her breasts, teasing the nipples to tautness.

"Do you like it when I do this?" he asked.

"Yes!"

Now he was stroking the delicate pyramids formed by her hip bones. "And this?"

"Oh, yes."

His hand moved to explore the shadowy mystery of her thighs, searching and probing with gently insistent thrusts of his fingers, penetrating deep and yet deeper until, at last, he found the soft, virginal essence of her.

"And here?"

Paige drew in a long, shuddering breath. She was moving restlessly, eager for more, instinctively responding to his lightest touch as he prepared her for the transition to womanhood. She hardly recognized her own voice as she cried, "Oh yes, Matt. Yes!"

Matt's face was suffused with passion as he folded her in his arms. He crushed her close to the full length of his body and the feel of his masculine hardness was deliciously exciting. She was overwhelmed by the need to be close to him and closer still; to absorb and possess him, to be possessed by him until their very spirits had merged.

There was an instant of wild, sweet pain; then he was invading secret, untouched places, giving her the most exquisite pleasure as they moved together, locked in a rhythm as old as time.

Sometimes, when she was alone in her room at night, Paige had dreamed of what it might be like if Matt were to make love to her, but never in her wildest fantasies had she dreamed that it would be like this—that she would feel this softening and yielding and melting and *wanting*. Her pleasure was so intense that it was very nearly unbearable. She was being enveloped by it, consumed by it, and she heard someone cry out. Only later did she realize that voice was her own.

Chapter Five

The dampness of tears on her cheeks brought Paige out of the near-trance her memories had induced. The seascape came back into focus, followed by the other impersonal details of the motel room, and she wiped the tears away impatiently with the back of one hand, wondering why she should be crying now when she hadn't cried for such a long time.

She hadn't wept since the baby, and even then she hadn't cried very much.

Her aunt had thought she was unfeeling, but the truth was that when the initial numbing shock had worn off, she had experienced a staggering onslaught of emotions.

In swift, punishing succession, she'd gone from disbelief and denial to despair, from anger and guilt to a despondency that was too deeply rooted to be dispelled by tears. And through it all, she couldn't eat, couldn't sleep, couldn't cry.

Her loyal friend Stella had cautioned against stoicism, but somehow, she hadn't been able to cry.

At the time she had felt that weeping would be an

overt admission that she had reason to grieve, and later she had been afraid that if she once started crying, she might never be able to stop. Besides, crying wouldn't repair the illusion that she could go through life without being touched by tragedy. All the tears in the world couldn't compensate for her loss.

At Stella's urging, after she'd moved to Mill Valley she'd made an appointment with a doctor. He'd said that she was young, that there was plenty of time, that she had her whole future ahead of her. In a misguided attempt to comfort her, he'd told her she could have other children.

But she had wanted Matt's child, and the future looked bleak. She wasn't certain she wanted to go on living. She'd wished she'd never been born.

She'd left the doctor's examining room and seen a number of his patients talking and laughing in the waiting room. While she'd waited for the receptionist to type out her bill, she'd studied them, envying them the serenity of their pregnancies, despising them for their complacency.

How could they laugh, she'd wondered, when life was so unfair? How could they feel serene in such a cruel world?

Paige wasn't sure how long she'd been trapped in that awful pit of despair. It might have been days or weeks. It might have been as long as several months. She knew only that one day she had decided the sensible thing would be to ignore her grief.

After this she'd sought oblivion in frenetic activity. She'd found a job and made a new life for herself. Time had dulled the sharpness of sorrow, but she'd known that she hadn't accepted her loss—not really.

For years, whenever she'd stopped to watch the children on the playground near her apartment, she'd wondered what her daughter would have been like at two years old, or three, or five. She'd asked herself if her little girl would have been sweet or sassy, a cherub or an imp. Would she have preferred to play with dolls or climb trees? Would she have had Matt's eyes? Would she have had his sense of adventure? Would she have had her mother's nose? Would she have been dark or fair? Would she have resembled this pink-and-white charmer or that scabby-kneed tomboy?

On occasions such as those, Paige thought that if she'd seen her baby, if she'd had the chance to hold her daughter in her arms—even for a little while—acceptance might have come more easily.

Then, as her business demanded more of her time and attention, as her involvement with community affairs grew and her circle of friends expanded, her preoccupation with such pointless, answerless questions had lessened. Her days were too full, her schedule too crowded to waste precious time dreaming of what might have been.

She hadn't stopped to watch the children in the playground for at least three years, but perhaps she still hadn't come to terms with her grief.

And when her aunt had died last December, once again she had been unable to cry.

Despite Aunt Rachel's remoteness, Paige had loved her, and she'd wanted to weep. She'd wanted to lament the rigidly circumscribed, Eleanor Rigby-like loneliness of Rachel Cavanaugh's life, but she had been composed and dry-eyed.

So why was she crying now?

Telling herself she was probably just overtired from the drive down the coast coupled with a nearly sleepless night, she glanced at her wristwatch. When she saw that it was nearly eight thirty, she thought, apathetically, that it was time to change clothes.

In a little more than half an hour, Matt would be arriving. She'd have to hurry if she didn't want to keep him waiting.

Making a selection at random, she pulled a blue shirtwaist dress out of her suitcase. She shook it once or twice and held it up in front of herself as she looked toward the mirror.

She had changed in the years since she'd last seen Matt, and although the changes went far deeper than surface appearances, it was her appearance that concerned her at this moment.

The starry-eyed, fresh-faced radiance she'd had as a teenager had given way to a more sober maturity. She was no longer so open, so trusting. The tilt of her chin proclaimed that, while she still hoped for the best, she tried to be prepared for the worst, and the expression in her eyes was more measuring than eager. But if she'd lost some of her eagerness to get on with the business of living, there was also a new assurance about her, a tranquil resignation that came from the knowledge that all things were *not* possible.

Would Matt approve of the way she'd changed? All at once it seemed terribly important to Paige that he should approve of her.

Swinging abruptly away from the mirror, she tossed the shirtwaist across the bed. She had to take most of the clothes out of the suitcase before she found the dress she wanted to wear: a full-skirted wraparound of fine, almost silky, wool in a cinnamon shade that emphasized the russet in her hair and the peach-bloom undertones in her skin.

Her hands were trembling with nervousness as, more hastily now, she searched for a change of underwear and the high-heeled pumps that went with the dress. Leaving the rest of her clothing heaped on the bed, she breathed a sigh of thanks for crushproof fabrics as she hurried toward the shower.

She was acutely aware of how cautiously she must handle the reunion with Matt. They had been friends for four months. They'd been lovers only for one night, but that night had brought them to this moment.

Since they were meeting under such trying circumstances, could their friendship be salvaged?

Perhaps. And if she could think of a graceful opening remark to get her through the stressful preliminaries when they met face to face, the idea of seeing Matt might seem less frightening. But what could she say to him that would strike the right note of friendly concern and affection?

A simple "Hello, how are you?" would not do at all, but what else could she say?

Paige agonized over this as she pulled off her clothes and tucked her hair into a plastic shower cap. No matter how she adjusted the taps, the water alternated from comfortably warm to incredibly frigid, and at last she gave up trying to regulate the temperature. She stepped beneath the spray, and while she soaped and rinsed, she tried out various greetings

"Thanks for coming by." Even as Paige spoke, she shook her head, discarding this overture.

"Thanks *so* much for coming by," she repeated the sentiment, attempting more warmth, and shook her head again. If the first was too casual, the second sounded as if she were gushing.

"It's been a long time." Too obvious. If she said something like that, Matt would probably tell her to go to hell and leave before she'd had a chance to explain.

"I've missed you." For all its glibness, this approach had one virtue. It was the truth. She *had* missed Matt, and with slight variations, this theme might work.

"I've thought of you often." For years she had thought of Matt every time she'd driven by a tennis court or golf course. Every time she'd seen a tall, dark-haired man. Every time she'd seen a child. She still thought of him on Thanksgiving and Christmas. Whenever she heard the Stanford fight song. Every time it rained—

"Your friendship meant more to me than I can say," Paige murmured, and silently added, *Please, let us still be friends.*

The water pressure had fallen to an icy trickle. The way her teeth were chattering made Paige more nervous than before, and she turned off the shower and wrapped herself in one of the thin, scratchy towels the motel provided.

As she got into her clothes she felt as if she'd sprouted an extra pair of thumbs, but in spite of her clumsiness, she was back in front of the mirror smoothing on lip gloss before she began to think of the ways in which Matt might have changed in the last eight years. And it was not until she heard his knock at the door that she wondered which Matt she was about to see.

Would he be friend or lover? Or, after all this time, would he seem like a stranger?

Shaken by the last possibility, Paige stared at the door.

Dear Lord! When she'd called Mrs. Jonas to get Matt's address, she hadn't even thought to ask if Matt was married. She was horrified by her oversight, although it seemed highly unlikely that he would have married. She couldn't imagine Matt giving up his freedom for any woman. But what if he had?

The knock came again, more sharply.

"Just a minute," Paige called.

She had started toward the door before she remembered that she'd left her clothes heaped on the bed. Without pausing to ask herself why this aberration should be so disturbing, she bundled the garments into her suitcase and shoved the case into the bathroom. Once that evidence was out of sight, she looked about the room for any other clues that might give away her panic.

Matt knocked again, this time impatiently.

"Coming," Paige called.

One of her nightgowns had fallen out of the suitcases, and she kicked it under the bed. With the flimsy garment disposed of, the room appeared to be in order, and she rushed to answer Matt's summons. But now her hands refused to cooperate. She fumbled with the knob for what seemed like hours before she finally managed to turn it, and the probing glance Matt gave her when she opened the door shattered the last remnant of her equanimity.

In some ways he's the same, thought Paige.

His hair was shorter than he'd worn it eight years ago, styled so that it was fuller around the temples, but it was as thick and dark as ever.

He, too, had matured. He'd grown into his rangy body. The youthful lankiness he'd had at twenty-seven was gone. He'd filled out and was more muscular, fitter, harder. His old arrogance had mellowed into easy self-confidence, but the set of his shoulders and the angle at which he held his jaw made it clear that he was aware of his rugged masculinity, and that he was proud of it.

How can he be so cool? Paige wondered. *Why did I keep him waiting? He must think I'm an idiot.*

She might almost have been transported back in time—to the dusky study in the Jonas house in Palo Alto, to the instant she'd first seen Matt—because she felt as unsure of herself as she had at eighteen.

Lord, she's cool! thought Matt. *How can she stand there, smiling politely, when all I can think of is kissing her?*

Both of them started to speak at once. "You're having your hair cut shorter these days," she observed while, at the same time, Matt said, "What, no T-shirt?"

They laughed and self-consciously lowered their eyes.

He's not wearing a wedding ring, thought Paige. *There are a million things I want to ask him, and one that I have to tell him.*

She's not wearing a wedding ring, thought Matt. *Why did she keep me waiting? Is she playing some sort of game?*

"You were saying?" she prompted.

"It wasn't important," said Matt. "You go first."

"I'll try, but I feel so foolish." Too flustered to dissemble, she confided, "You see, I had this whole speech planned but now my mind's a total blank and I don't know where to begin."

"Would it help if I told you I hate listening to speeches?"

"Yes," said Paige. "I remember you do."

"Then why did you prepare one?"

"I wanted to impress you."

Matt smiled. "You have impressed me, Irish," he said softly. "Probably more than you realize."

His candor should have broken the ice, but it didn't. In her uneasiness, Paige was stiff and formal during the exchange of meaningless pleasantries that followed. Yet when Matt held her elbow to guide her to his car, she felt an alarmingly familiar tingle at the touch of his hand.

She studied him in the lights from the oncoming traffic as they drove away from the motel, and it was then that she saw how much he had changed.

His face was leaner, tougher. His skin was sun-bronzed and unlined, tautly stretched over the strong bones of his face, and it occurred to Paige that this Matt might be more than a little ruthless if he were crossed.

She quickly looked away from him. Her hands felt clammy and she smoothed them along her skirt and tucked them into the pockets of the jacket she had thrown over her shoulders. Only gradually did she become aware that Matt was speaking to her.

"... and since you stressed that you prefer to talk privately," he was saying, "I thought we'd go to my place."

"Th-that's fine."

Paige closed her eyes and gritted her teeth, trying to quell the quavering weakness that assailed her at the sound of his voice.

My reaction to him hasn't changed, she acknowledged silently, *and, damn it, I wish it had!*

She shoved her hands deeper into her jacket pockets and the fingers of one hand came into contact with the envelope that contained the newspaper clipping. This was enough to strengthen her resolve, for it served as a reminder of her purpose in seeing Matt.

Feeling more in command of herself, Paige opened her eyes and saw that they were driving along a palm-lined, ocean-front boulevard. To their left the Pacific stretched endlessly toward the horizon. The Channel Islands were out there somewhere, lost in the darkness.

In a pool of artificial light just ahead was the yacht basin, where commercial fishing boats rubbed brawny shoulders with sleek power cruisers, and oceangoing sailboats bobbed at their moorings, their tall masts swaying as they hobnobbed with modest day-sailers.

From its hillside above the harbor, the City College, ablaze with lights, looked down upon the marina.

"I should congratulate you on your column," said Paige, stealing a glance at Matt out of the corner of her eye. "I was impressed by the piece you did on industrial espionage. It was very...hard-hitting."

"Thanks. It was intended to be."

When Matt glanced over at her, she avoided his gaze. They were approaching one of the fine old adobe buildings that were sprinkled around the city, and she studied it curiously, waiting until they had passed it before she asked, "Why did you decide to live in Santa Barbara?"

"Why not? It's fairly centrally located. It's an easy drive to L.A., San Diego, or San Francisco, and it's where everyone wants to come for their vacation."

"*That's* why not. It's—I don't know. It's so conscious of its own attractions—so darned smug! And it's too perfect to be real. It looks like a movie set."

"What you're saying is that you'd like the town better if it had some faults," Matt said dryly.

"Well, what's wrong with that? You're the one who taught me that faults can be endearing."

When she turned to look at Matt again, she saw that he was smiling.

"I see you haven't lost your touch with backhanded compliments," he observed.

"You know what I mean! Don't you ever get tired of perennial sunshine and blue skies and palm trees?"

"No, Irish, I can't say that I do. But Santa Barbara's not perfect. You get tar all over your feet on the beaches hereabouts."

Paige wrinkled her nose disdainfully. "Big deal!"

"Picky, picky, picky," Matt retorted, scolding her mildly.

His grin broadened. Then he began to chuckle, and after a few seconds, Paige joined him, laughing because they'd unconsciously fallen into their comfortable old habit of good-natured squabbling. It seemed that their friendship was not beyond redemption after all, and Paige's spirits rose. *It's going to be all right,* she thought.

"So tell me," said Matt, "have you succumbed to the lure of the big city, or do you still call Alder Creek home?"

Paige smiled at his reference to her hometown. Alder Creek was so small, the town proper consisted of nothing more than a combination general store and two-pump gas station, and the post office where her Aunt Rachel had worked.

"I'm living in Mill Valley now,' she replied, "but compared to Alder Creek, it seems like a metropolis."

"Is your job in San Francisco then?"

"No. I work in Mill Valley, too. I have my own small business."

"As a consultant?"

"Hardly," she said lightly. "I contract to take care of the window displays for a number of small, independently owned stores in the area."

"Why aren't you doing research?"

"Because I never finished college."

Matt's jaw dropped with astonishment. There was a moment of shocked silence.

"Oh, no," he exclaimed softly. "What a waste!"

"I'm sorry if you're disappointed, but I don't think it's a waste at all. For major holidays and the change of seasons, some of my clients contract with me to coordinate all of their decorations, so my work is challenging and it offers variety and the chance to be creative. I enjoy it. Furthermore, I'm pretty damned good at it."

"I've no doubt that you are, Irish. It's just that I assumed you'd be involved with some kind of research. When you were at Stanford, you were all wrapped up in that project of yours—something to do with fungus, wasn't it?"

"The effect, if any, of electromagnetic fields on certain types of mold," Paige recited tonelessly. "And, yes, I found it intriguing. I know everyone expected me to continue in that vein or some related field. Heaven knows everyone encouraged me! My aunt nearly disowned me when I dropped out of school. But I never wanted that for myself. Just the idea of being shut away in a lab gave me the shivers. I'd had enough of books. I wanted to be involved with people."

"I can appreciate that," said Matt.

"I should think you would, especially since you were the self-appointed, one-man entertainment committee for anything in skirts—"

"Hey, come on now! I was more discriminating than that."

"I know," she agreed pertly. "They had to be female, reasonably attractive, and between the ages of twenty and thirty—"

"Sometimes they were younger," Matt asserted smoothly.

Paige caught her lower lip between her teeth. She regretted that she'd given him this opening for it threatened to disrupt their fragile camaraderie. But Matt didn't belabor the issue. Instead he changed the subject.

"I ran into a friend of yours last week—Maida Ormond."

"Did you?" Paige replied slowly. "I haven't seen Maida in years. How is she?"

"Fine. The same. She's teaching at Sacramento State. But how about Jay What's-his-name? Do you still see him?"

"His last name is Lowndes, and yes, I see him fairly often. Jay and his wife are both good friends of mine."

Matt had sounded as if he were testing her, but because it was too dark to see his expression, she couldn't be sure. Now that they had reached the outskirts of the city, they'd left the freeway behind. They were traveling along a narrow, twisting lane that led in the general direction of the ocean, and the only source of light was the reflected glow of the dashboard.

"And how about you?" she added. "Do you ever see Carole What's-her-name?"

"Only when she's between husbands," Matt replied in a faintly aggrieved tone. "Which proves that I do have some scruples."

"I know you do," Paige admitted contritely. "You're one of the most honorable men I've ever met."

As he spun the wheel, turning from the lane onto an even narrower private drive, Matt acknowledged her apology, declaring in a sardonic drawl, "Well, Irish, you should know."

There's no denying that, Paige thought grimly. After the night they had spent together, Matt had tried to do the right thing by her. He'd even offered to marry her, and when she had refused, he'd been frustrated and angry; not because he loved her, but because her refusal had constituted a direct attack upon his sense of honor.

She was grateful they had arrived at Matt's house, for his preoccupation with collecting the past week's mail from the box at the foot of the driveway made it unnecessary for her to come up with a response to his statement.

He parked the car near the house and stopped to retrieve his attaché case and a suitcase from the trunk before he came around to the passenger side to open her door.

The sighing sound of the surf told her the ocean was just beyond the next ridge of sand dunes as she followed him up the walk toward the entryway. Safe in her refuge of silence, she surveyed the house as she went.

Matt's home came as a surprise to Paige. In this area where Spanish or Moorish architecture were the order of the day, the last thing she had expected was its refreshing contemporary simplicity. Its two levels were built long and low, so that the house seemed an integral part of its site, while its roof line and the use of sand-colored brick and natural wood in its facade whispered subtly of the Orient.

Inside, Matt guided her along a hallway that ran the length of the house, up a flight of stairs, and into the living room.

"I went straight to the office from the airport, so if you'll excuse me for a few minutes, I'll just take a look at my mail." Waving toward the bar, he said, "Help yourself to a drink if you want one, and look around all you like."

Left alone, Paige took Matt at his word and sauntered about the living room. It was decorated predominantly in palest champagne, with accents of tobacco brown occasionally spiced by sharp citrus shades. The room was beautifully proportioned, a pleasing mixture of textures and patterns, light and shadow, airy open spaces and private coziness. The overall effect was one of the blending of its parts into an harmonious entity.

The draperies were drawn across the window wall, but she knew there would be a deck behind them, and that the windows offered a spectacular view of the ocean.

With the clues provided by some of the delightful things the room contained, Paige found she could map Matt's travels as a correspondent. There was Czechoslovakian crystal, Italian porcelain, and a pair of cloissoné vases from mainland China. There were English hunting prints, and a camel saddle of finely tooled Moroccan leather. And from its own lighted recess near the fireplace, the statue of the goddess

Kuan Yin, which Paige had last seen in Dr. Jonas's study, smiled down upon the room.

After spending some time renewing her acquaintance with the figurine, Paige wandered to the other side of the living room in order to take a closer look at a cluster of photographs on the wall near the stereo. She was engrossed with them when Matt returned.

As he folded back the louvered doors at the base of the built-in bar, revealing a small refrigerator, he said, "Sorry to keep you waiting. I took the time to start the steaks broiling."

He'd also taken time to change from his business suit to a pair of comfortably faded jeans and a cotton knit sport shirt that fitted him like a second skin.

"May I take your jacket now that the house is warm?" he inquired.

"I—I think I'll keep it on a little longer," she stammered guiltily. She wanted to have easy access to the clipping when the time came to tell Matt about her mission and ask for his help.

As he handed her a glass of white wine, Matt gave her a telling glance that made it clear he thought she was behaving oddly. Aloud, however, all he said was, "To old friends."

"Old friends," she echoed.

They clinked glasses, and after she'd taken a sip of wine to seal the toast, she ventured, "Do you know, this house is really lovely."

Matt winced. "You needn't sound so surprised, but thanks anyway. It's not entirely my doing, though. These days I can afford to hire a housekeeper, and a friend of mine took care of furnishing the place."

With the hand that held her wineglass, Paige indicated the silver-framed photograph at the very center of the grouping she'd been studying. The picture showed Matt cavorting on the beach with a stunning blond woman.

"Is she the friend who did the decorating?"

"Yes, she is."

Paige opened her mouth to speak. Then, changing her mind, she took another sip of wine.

"What were you going to say?" asked Matt.

"Just that you're still the same old Matt, but if your friend has been around long enough to decorate your house for you, you've changed."

"Not so much that I'm unrecognizable, I trust."

"No, not to that extent. I'd have known you—anywhere."

Matt's wide grin eased the strain she felt for having said something so revealing. "What about you, Irish? Have you changed? Do you still wear T-shirts with slogans printed all over the front?"

Paige smiled wryly and shook her head. "I hope I'm a little less opinionated now—and a lot less obvious. I think I might have a couple of old T-shirts kicking around my apartment somewhere, but they're fairly bland, and I haven't worn one in ages."

"I'm sorry to hear that. I always looked forward to seeing what you'd come up with next. My personal favorite was the one that said 'If I can't dance to it, it's not my revolution,' but I must say I admired your lack of vanity when you wore the one that had 'Reese's Peanut Butter Cups' printed in strategic places."

"I hate to disillusion you, but lack of vanity had nothing to do with it. I wore that one out of ignorance. Some of the women in my dorm gave me the shirt, and I never even realized they were playing a practical joke on me until I'd worn it several times."

"From what your jacket allows me to see of you, there's at least one way you've changed. That Reese's shirt would be false advertising now." Matt's eyes traveled slowly, significantly, to her breasts. "Come to think of it, if my memory serves me correctly, it was false advertising then."

Paige didn't know how to reply to that. To cover her discomfiture, she lifted her glass to her lips to take another sip of wine, but her hand was shaking so badly that some of the liquid sloshed onto her jacket. As she brushed ineffectually at the damp spot on the cream-colored linen, Matt chuckled, pleased because his comment had found its mark.

"You've never learned how to flirt, have you?" he said with annoying cheerfulness. "Here, let me take your jacket."

"No! Really, it's all right. What harm can a little white wine do?" She slipped the jacket off her shoulders. "I'll just hang it over the back of this chair and it will dry in no time."

Glancing frantically around the room for something that might divert Matt from his determination to relieve her of her jacket, she spotted the Chinese figurine and remarked brightly, "I see you have your mother's *Kuan Yin*. She looks right at home here."

Matt turned to look toward the goddess. "I think Mom's decided her hints aren't doing the trick and it's going to take some kind of miracle before I'll present her with grandchildren.''

Paige's heart leaped into her throat at his reference to children. "H-how is your mother, Matt?" she inquired, hoping that he would attribute her stammer to her very real concern for Eve Jonas's health. "When I talked to Dr. Jonas, he said she'd had a stroke."

"She did," Matt replied. "Last year. She's able to talk almost normally now, but there's still quite a bit of weakness on the left side of her body so she doesn't get around very well. She's accepted her condition philosophically, and she's learned to live within her limitations. The last time I spoke to her she told me you'd called to ask for my address, by the way. She was delighted to hear from you after such a long silence."

"I'm sorry I didn't keep in touch," Paige said softly. "I always admired your mother. If anyone could make a good adjustment to a chronic illness, it would be her. It must be hard on Dr. Jonas, though, seeing her that way. And on you."

Except to move his shoulders as if he were shrugging off her sympathy, Matt made no response to this. When a buzzer sounded from the direction of the kitchen, he announced it was the oven timer.

"It's time to turn the steak," he explained as he strode toward the hall. "My housekeeper left a salad in the refrigerator, so dinner will be ready in a few minutes."

Chapter Six

Forty-five minutes later they were sitting at the butcher-block table in the kitchen. Matt was eating with his usual gusto, while Paige had taken only a small serving of salad and barely managed to get that down.

As he carved a third helping of steak for himself, Matt inquired, "Are you sure you don't want some of this?"

"I'm positive," Paige replied adamantly. Just the sight of the steak made her want to shudder. It was charred on the outside and practically raw on the inside.

"Some wine then?" Matt suggested. "There's just enough left in the bottle for both of us to have one more glass."

"Thanks." Paige held out her half-full glass and Matt refilled it and his own.

When he had finished pouring the wine, he saw the wary way she was looking at his steak and smiled.

"I see you've noticed I still like my steak blood-rare."

Returning his smile, she admitted, "I could hardly miss noticing that. In that respect, you're the same old Matt."

"Have you ever stopped to ask yourself why I wouldn't be?" His grin broadened. "I mean, why would I want to tamper with perfection?"

"You're still modest too!"

"Well, Irish, as I used to tell you, there are two kinds of people in this world: Those who have good reason to be modest—" Matt raised his hands like an orchestra conductor cuing one of his musicians; he signaled Paige and, in unison, they shouted, "And those who don't!"

Paige broke into an earthy, rollicking cascade of laughter that both surprised and pleased her. It made her realize how long it had been since she'd really laughed.

"Good heavens, but that takes me back!" she exclaimed. "I wish I'd kept a record of all the homilies you taught me. You had one for every occasion. Talk about the power of positive thinking! You should write them all down and sell them with a money-back guarantee if they don't chase away the blahs!"

Her laughter tapered to a tentative smile when she saw that Matt was studying her soberly.

"A while ago I asked if you've changed, but you never did answer me." He quirked an eyebrow at her. "How about it, Irish? Are you still the same?"

"I still don't like raw meat, if that's what you mean," she answered stiltedly.

"No, that's not what I mean."

Paige sighed resignedly. "In some ways I'm the same. I still want the same things from life."

"How have you managed to keep some guy from dragging you to the altar?"

"You're forgetting, I had lessons from the champ."

"So you did," Matt acknowledged, "but just because it was right for me to stay single, it doesn't necessarily follow that it's the best thing for you. I realize the last time I saw you, you were too enamored of your freedom to consider marriage, but I always thought that eventually you'd want to go the husband and home route."

"Right down to the white picket fence," she said without thinking. "The station wagon, the beagle—"

"And the kids," Matt finished softly.

Here it was, thought Paige. The opening she'd been waiting for. She devoutly hoped that the combination of wine, reminiscence, and a hearty meal would make Matt receptive to what she had to ask of him.

"That's what I wanted to discuss with you," she said evenly. "First, though, there's something I'd like to show you by way of explanation." She pushed her chair away from the table and got to her feet. "It's in the other room—"

"In your jacket pocket," Matt hazarded.

"Y-yes. I'll just go and get it."

"Please do."

Paige wanted to run, but she forced herself to walk until she had left the kitchen. Then she scurried along the hall, up the stairs and into the living room. After retrieving the envelope, she removed the clipping and ran back the way she'd come. Just outside the kitchen, she stopped to take a few deep breaths and compose herself. When she re-entered the room, she walked steadily to the table, resumed her seat, and handed Matt the article.

She was dismayed when, after the most cursory inspection of the clipping, Matt began to chuckle. Looking up at her, he said, "You really had me going for a minute there."

Confused, Paige shook her head. "I don't understand."

"You've got to be putting me on! After the way you've groused about my cooking, you can't seriously expect me to whip up"—Matt looked at the clipping again before he concluded—"Ah, yes—'roast duckling with orange glaze.'"

Paige smiled weakly. "No, Matt. The article I'd like you to read is on the other side."

She watched Matt closely, trying to gauge his reaction as he turned the clipping over and began reading the article. If she'd had to, she could have recited it to him. She had read it so many times, she'd memorized it.

It began with a picture of an infant; a picture that was grainy and slightly out of focus, as if the baby had moved in the same instant the camera lens opened. She could visualize the caption. It read: "Do you know this baby?"

The story itself wasn't very long. It told about a Mrs. Ralph Johnson who had found a newborn girl in the ladies' room of a local movie theater. "The poor wee thing hardly had strength enough to cry," Mrs. Johnson was quoted as saying. "And she's so tiny;

almost like a little doll." The story closed with the request that anyone with information about the baby or her parents phone the sheriff's office at the county courthouse.

Matt read the article through twice. The first time his brows were knitted with perplexity. He darted an occasional glance at Paige, as if he were puzzling over her connection with the story. By the second time, he was scowling, and when he put the clipping down on the table, his eyes were smoldering with barely suppressed fury.

"Earlier you stressed the personal nature of your business with me," he said coldly. "I take it that, in one way or another, the baby referred to in the article is involved."

Paige nodded. In a nearly inaudible voice, she said, "She's mine."

"Come again?" Matt snapped. "I didn't hear you."

Paige cleared her throat. Lifting her chin proudly, she repeated, "She's mine—at least, she might be."

"I can't believe I'm hearing this," Matt muttered angrily. "Why is it so difficult for you to admit the baby is yours? Are you ashamed because she was born out of wedlock? Is that why you abandoned her? Was it the old like mother, like daughter cliché?"

"I'm not ashamed, and I didn't abandon her, damn it! On the contrary, I'm hoping to find her. The only reason it's hard for me to tell you about her is that I'm worried about how you might react."

"How *I* might react! Why the hell would you—"

Matt stopped in midsentence to stare at Paige. She saw the dawning comprehension in the speculative

way his eyes narrowed, in the way his mouth thinned
to a bitter line.

"You were afraid to tell me because I'm the *father*!
My God! You lied about that too!"

He slammed his fist down on the corner of the
table so forcefully that he felt the jarring impact of
the blow at the base of his skull. The dishes rattled
and Paige jumped. Then, as if his fury required further expression, he lunged to his feet and began
stalking back and forth, pacing the length of the
kitchen.

Paige honestly didn't blame Matt for being angry.
Thanks to the months she'd spent with Stella Ackerman, she understood his reaction. And since she'd
seen him in a similar mood eight years ago, when his
injuries had prevented his returning to work and he'd
found himself in a situation over which he'd had no
control, she had even anticipated it.

Even so, his condemnation was hard to bear. His
taunt about her mother had struck a nerve, and she
resented his last accusation.

She had never lied to Matt about anything. Admittedly, she might have shaded the truth a bit over
some issues, and she had knowingly misled him about
her pregnancy, but she had never actually lied to him.
Not even about that.

About six weeks after the night they'd been together, on a raw early February day, Matt had paid her
a surprise visit at her Aunt Rachel's home. He'd
claimed he was just passing through, that he was on
his way to visit a colleague in Sacramento, but she'd
known this was a ruse for the simple reason that Alder

Creek wasn't on the way to anywhere. It was a dead-end.

Besides, even though he'd skirted the matter, she knew why he'd come. The question he'd wanted to ask hung between them, forming a barrier that made both of them uneasy.

All in all, they had spent about two hours together that day, and for the first time they were uncomfortable with one another. Their attempts at conversation were so awkward that, out of desperation, Paige suggested they take a walk down to the creek.

Although it was the height of the rainy season, the grass-covered foothills were sere and brown. The creekbed was dry, but that was not unusual. Alder Creek had changed course years before, after a flood.

When she'd told Matt this, he'd inquired, "Was that by any chance *the* flood?" And when she hadn't laughed at his attempt at humor, he'd said, "You know, the Biblical one with Noah and all the gang—"

"I know the one you mean," she'd replied waspishly. "I'm not that much of a hick. Alder Creek might be remote, but we are familiar with the Bible. It's just that it all happened before my time, so I can't say for sure." After pausing briefly, she'd added, "You won't find any alders hereabouts either, only a few scrubby old oak trees, and they're stunted from all the mistletoe that's growing on them."

For a long moment Matt had stared at her, and she'd berated herself for not laughing at his quip. After all, she had started the whole business of poking fun at the tiny rural community by telling him that even the creek hadn't wanted to stay in the town that was its namesake. Then, when he had responded in kind, she'd gone all defensive.

She knew he was wondering why, if she disliked the place so much, she hadn't returned to Stanford when classes had resumed after the semester break. Because she didn't have a convincing explanation to give him, she'd been afraid he might ask her this. But he hadn't.

Instead he'd told her that his doctor had released him from treatment and that he was scheduled to leave for Bucharest at the end of the month. He'd talked quite a lot about his new assignment, but she hadn't paid much attention to what he'd said. She'd been impressed by his eagerness to get back to work, but mostly she'd looked at him and listened to the sound of his beautiful voice, avidly storing up images of him to help fill the loneliness after he'd gone. She'd wished she had a photograph of him—even a snapshot.

Finally, when he was preparing to leave, he'd asked, "Are you all right, Irish?"

"I'm fine, Matt," she'd answered, relieved that he hadn't asked her point blank if she was pregnant. Because by then, of course, she'd known that she was. What's more, she was happy about it. She had cherished the knowledge that if she couldn't have Matt, at least she would have his child.

She'd known that eventually she would have to tell Matt about the baby, but just then she hadn't the strength to deny him if he'd proposed marriage again, and she'd thought she had time.

Later, she'd promised herself, after the baby was

born, she would write to Matt and tell him about his child.

Thinking that her youthful faith in the future had been sadly misplaced, Paige ruefully shook her head.

She glanced obliquely at Matt. His face was still set and hard, but he was pacing more slowly. Maybe now he was prepared to listen to reason. She took a fortifying swallow of wine, and the next time he passed the table, she caught hold of his arm.

He glared at her irately, but he didn't pull away. Meeting his gaze squarely, she said, "Matt, I swear I didn't abandon the baby. I was led to believe she was stillborn."

For a full minute he stared down at her, measuring the validity of her statement. At last, he said quietly, "I'll accept that." Returning to his chair, he sat astride it, facing her. "You'd better tell me the rest of it."

"Well," she began a bit shakily, "the first thing you should know is that I found the clipping about a month ago—"

"Wrong! The first thing I should know is whether you knew you were pregnant when I came to see you before I left for Rumania."

"Yes, I knew." Paige made the admission defiantly. When Matt opened his mouth to make some comment, she rushed on, "I didn't lie about it. You never asked me if I was pregnant. You only asked if I was all right."

"But you were aware of what I really wanted to know."

"Naturally I was."

"So why did you keep the truth from me? Was it the idea of marriage that was repugnant to you, or was it me that turned you off?"

"Please, Matt, can't we go into this later?"

"Later!" Matt exclaimed explosively. "It's eight years after the fact, and you think you can palm me off with *later*?"

"I'm not trying to palm you off with anything, but if we go into our personal motivations at this stage, we're ignoring what's important *now*." When she saw that Matt had not been swayed by her logic, Paige added coolly, "Anyway, you could have asked me straight out if I was pregnant. Since you didn't, I might just as easily suggest that you failed to put the question more directly to leave yourself an escape hatch."

"Do you honestly believe that?" Matt demanded.

Her eyes shied away from his. "I'm not sure what I believe. All I know is that there's a possibility Aunt Rachel lied to me, and if my baby is alive—"

"*Our* baby," Matt said curtly.

Paige's shoulders sagged at this correction, "Our baby," she agreed numbly. Apparently Matt decided she was properly chastened, because he waited for her to go on. "If she's alive, I have to find her."

"And what then?"

Paige passed one hand over her eyes, bewildered by the question. She was trembling inside, and she knew her fragile control might give way at any minute.

"I don't know what you mean. Either she's alive or she's "—unable to make herself say the word, Paige haltingly substituted—"or she isn't."

"Suppose she is alive? Suppose she's been adopted and she's been part of a family all these years? What then? Do you plan to make some sort of claim on the parents as her biological mother? Would you go so far as to uproot her? What I want to know is, is it her you're concerned about, or is it yourself?"

At his question about making claims, Paige began shaking her head, and with each succeeding question her denial became more strenuous, more desperate. *Dear heaven,* she thought, *does Matt truly think I'm capable of that kind of selfishness?*

In a choked voice, Paige cried, "If she's alive and happily situated, that would be more than I've dared hope for, but I have to know! Oh, Matt, don't you see? That's all I want. To know!"

Her appeal was so impassioned that finally, grudgingly, Matt was convinced. He reached across the table and touched her hand. When she did not respond, he gave her hand a sympathetic squeeze and she turned her palm toward his, returning the warm pressure of his fingers.

"Will you listen to me now?" she asked.

"I'll listen," he said crisply. "Make your pitch."

His flippancy left room for Paige to doubt his sincerity, and she launched into the story hesitantly.

"You—uh, you met my Aunt Rachel," she said.

Matt nodded. Recalling the prim, stern-visaged woman Paige had introduced him to that day at Alder Creek, he remarked, "I don't imagine she was very supportive when she found out you were pregnant."

"She was supportive enough about that," Paige replied. "Actually, Aunt Rachel was more upset when I told her I wasn't going back to college. When I was little she'd had to put up with a lot of nasty comments about my...parentage. As a result, she had this terrible need for vindication. I guess she thought if I achieved something really fantastic, that would show everyone the errors of their ways in being so petty.

"When I told her I was pregnant, her first reaction was to urge me to put the baby up for adoption, but when I refused even to consider doing that, she didn't press the issue. She did ask me to leave town though. She said she'd already had all she could take of sanctimonious busybodies washing her family's dirty linen in public. I could appreciate why she felt like that, so I agreed to go away."

"Where did you go?" asked Matt.

"I stayed with an old friend of Aunt Rachel's—Stella Ackerman. In those days, Stella lived in the mother-lode country, about twenty miles from Sonora. She had a kennel and she bred and raised Saint Bernards. She was a professional handler as well—you know, she'd put dogs through their paces in the show ring—so she had to be away from the kennel most weekends, traveling around to the different shows. I helped out by taking care of the kennel while she was gone."

A nostalgic smile lifted the corners of Paige's mouth and restored some of the sunshine to her eyes. "In some respects, Stella was decidedly odd. She wasn't very tall, but she had this big, booming voice, and she dressed eccentrically, usually in a man's shirt and twill pants and knee boots. She'd march around the yard barking out commands to her dogs, and sometimes she'd talk to me the same way. She'd say, 'Sit, Paige! Eat, Paige!'"

"She sounds formidable," Matt said dryly.

"She was in a way, but the funny thing was that the dogs never paid any attention to her commands unless it suited them to obey her. And there was a tender side to Stella, too. By training, she was a nurse-midwife, so if one of the Saint Bernards was hurt or sick, she took care of it herself. And several times she brought home a fox or a raccoon or some other small animal that she'd rescued from a trap. In most cases, they were injured too badly to survive, but she treated them too, and when they didn't recover, she was outraged. She'd rant and rave, and slam around the place—"

"Her way of handling grief," Matt observed.

Paige nodded.

"You were very fond of her, weren't you, Irish?"

"Yes, I was. Stella didn't have much use for most people, but she was pretty wonderful to me. In fact, I don't know what I'd have done..." Paige left the rest of the sentence dangling. With an apologetic shake of her head, she said, "I'm sorry I'm rambling so."

"Don't worry—you know damned well I'll tell you if I'm bored."

Paige found Matt's bluntness reassuring, but she promised herself she would not get sidetracked again.

"Stella was away on one of her show circuits when I went into labor," she disclosed, remembering the pandemonium that had awakened her from a restless sleep on that moonless August night. She filled Matt in on the circumstances that had surrounded the baby's birth quickly, without digression. She was spar-ing with details to the point of sounding detached, but even so, in talking about that night, she relived much of it.

She had gone to bed early that night because she wasn't feeling well. Although her body had undergone the changes usually associated with pregnancy, until the past few days she hadn't felt pregnant. Lately, however, she felt clumsy and uncomfortable and so heavy that even the smallest chore seemed to require too much exertion. She was tired all the time, but it was impossible to sleep because she was plagued by a nebulous assortment of aches and pains.

All that day, for instance, she'd had a dull ache in the small of her back. She'd tried sitting, standing, walking, and lying down, but the ache had refused to go away. And now, just when she'd gotten to sleep, all hell had broken loose out in the kennel.

From the noise the dogs were making, they were in a frenzy over something or other, so she didn't even stop to put on a robe before she went outside to check on them, hurrying as much as her unwieldy shape and the uneven ground would permit.

The overpowering smell of skunk alerted her to part of the problem long before she arrived at the kennel building. She held her breath as she covered the final few yards to the kennel, and before she opened the door, she clamped her hand over her nose and mouth, trying to minimize the nauseating effect of the odor.

When she went inside and switched on the lights, the first thing she saw was the intruder—a skunk that had wandered into the run nearest the door. In spite of the noise and the stench, she immediately realized that the skunk was not behaving normally. For all the potency of its natural defense mechanism, it should have been retreating from the two full-grown Saint Bernards that occupied the run, not advancing on them.

Recently the County Health Department had issued warnings about an outbreak of rabies in the rodent population, and Paige recognized the danger. She also recognized the necessity of summoning aid. Much as she wanted to help the dogs, she was not about to try to capture a rabid skunk single-handed—or for that matter, an unrabid skunk.

The barking of the dogs reached its zenith when she left the kennel, and she tried to run. For the moment the dogs were cautiously avoiding the skunk, so the confrontation in the kennel was at a stalemate, but she didn't know how long the dogs might be expected to hold their own against the animal.

She had taken no more than ten steps when she fell, heavily, painfully, tumbling over and over down the steep incline that bordered the path, gathering momentum as she fell, like a snowball rolling downhill.

She landed at the bottom of the gully, her head striking a boulder. Fortunately it was only a glancing blow, but it was enough to cause her to lose consciousness. She had no idea how long she'd been out before she came to. The dogs had stopped barking, and only the silence told her of the passage of time.

She was confused and not immediately aware of the

gravity of her predicament. When she eased to a sitting position, she was assailed by nausea and dizziness, and when she tried to stand, she realized her right ankle was either badly sprained or broken.

Later she would wonder whether she had simply twisted her ankle on the trail, or if it was the grinding pain in her back that had caused her to stumble.

She started working her way up the slope toward the path. Because of her ankle, she was reduced to scrabbling along on her hands and knees, but she was almost amused by the ridiculousness of her plight until the pain occurred again. This time it was worse than before; wrenching and piercing, sharp enough that she lost her precarious hold on the bank and slid back down to the bottom of the slope.

From that point, her memories were mercifully hazy. Her ordeal had become a nightmare of pain and fear and desolation. Her mind wandered in and out of consciousness, and during the fleeting minutes she was conscious, the night seemed endless.

She battled against awareness, and eventually she found solace by imagining that Matt was with her. She was comforted by her visions of him. As the periods of lucidity decreased the images of Matt became more real to her than the pain or the sullen oppressive sky above her or the stony ground on which she lay.

Toward dawn a light rain began to fall, but she remembered nothing of that. She knew only that one minute she felt as if she were burning up, and the next she was shaken by chills.

It was mid-morning before Stella got home and found Paige. Afterward she told Paige that somehow she had managed to make it up to the path and almost to the house. In her concern with treating Paige's other injuries, Stella had not immediately recognized that Paige was in labor.

As the crow flies, the distance between Alder Creek and Stella Ackerman's kennel was not a great one, but because the roads were so bad, Rachel Cavanaugh did not arrive at her friend's home until early afternoon—only a scant half hour before Paige was delivered of a baby girl.

The baby was seven weeks premature. She was tiny, but she was perfectly formed and very beautiful. She was also stillborn—or so Rachel Cavanaugh had always maintained.

Chapter Seven

"Let's see if I've got this straight," said Matt when Paige had reached the end of her story. With angry jabs of the fingers of one hand, he began ticking off some of the things she'd told him.

"You'd had a fall so you were probably concussed. You'd hurt your ankle, you were suffering from exposure and then you developed what sounds like pneumonia. On top of all that, you'd just given birth, and *you're telling me your aunt never bothered to call a doctor?* My God, Irish! Didn't you think that was at all suspicious?"

"Well, as I said, Stella was a nurse-midwife—"

"But they never once called a doctor," Matt insisted.

"They may have called one. I was pretty much out of it for a couple of weeks."

"But you don't recall seeing one."

"No," Paige conceded. "The first time I recall seeing a doctor was after I'd left Stella's and gone to the Bay Area."

"And you never actually saw the baby?"

"No. They showed me her grave though. It was in the family plot on Stella's property, on a little knoll, with pine trees all around. It was a lovely spot. They'd put in a marker." Her voice broke on the last words. Her throat ached with unshed tears.

"A do-it-yourself funeral," Matt muttered. "And since there was no doctor involved, there'd be no death certificate."

"No, there wasn't," Paige confirmed. She had already checked that possibility.

"I'd be interested to know how you explained all this to yourself at the time," Matt drawled sarcastically.

"Do you think I might be right then?" Paige asked eagerly. "About Aunt Rachel lying, I mean?"

"I didn't say that. It's just that I find it hard to believe you didn't question the way Stella and your aunt avoided notifying the proper authorities."

"Oh." The glow of eagerness in Paige's eyes faded so swiftly, it was as if an inner light had been extinguished. "Well, I knew why Stella wouldn't want anyone coming around."

"So enlighten me," Matt directed.

"It was because of the skunk, you see. The dogs had killed it, but it had bitten one of them. I don't know why, perhaps it was because she disliked anyone dictating how she should run her business, but Stella's Saint Bernards had never been vaccinated for rabies. If it turned out the skunk was rabid, and if anyone had found out about it, her dogs could have been quarantined for as long as a year. Stella isolated the dog the skunk had bitten, but she didn't want to have all her dogs put under quarantine. She derived quite a bit of her income from stud fees, and be-sides—"

"Okay, I get the picture." Matt sighed gustily. "From what you've told me about Stella, that makes a certain amount of sense. And I can understand why you think your aunt might have believed lying was the best thing she could do for you, but that still leaves one question. Why would Stella lie about the baby?"

With a weary shake of her head Paige said, "I just don't know, Matt. I've done a lot of thinking about that since I found the clipping, but unless she was in-fluenced by the ideas of her generation a great deal more than she ever let on, I simply can't explain why she'd lie about a thing like that."

"Neither can I." Almost as an afterthought, Matt conjectured, "Unless your aunt forced Stella to go along with the lie in return for keeping Stella's secret about the rabies."

"I never thought of that!" Paige cried elatedly. "Oh, Matt, do you think that's what happened?"

"Take it easy, Irish," Matt calmly advised. "It's too soon to get your hopes up. You mentioned you were unable to locate Stella."

Paige nodded. "I sent her a letter, and when it was returned, I tried phoning her. But she's no longer listed in the Sonora phone book."

"You haven't seen her since then?"

"No, I haven't. And I didn't find any letters from her among my aunt's papers. I talked to the post-master in Sonora, and he told me she'd sold her kennel. He recalled it was quite a few years ago, but I don't even know when she left the area."

"You don't even know if she's still alive," Matt added, "so what you're left with is this."

He tapped the clipping with his forefinger in an impatient, dismissive gesture. Then he picked up the article and examined it more closely.

"It's not much to go on. There's no dateline, nothing to identify the newspaper that ran it. Hell! It's such a poor piece of reporting, it doesn't even specify which county to contact with information."

"I—I thought you might know of some way of identifying the newspaper," Paige stammered.

Tossing the article disgustedly aside, Matt leaned away from the back of his chair and folded his arms across his chest.

"Sorry, Irish, but as far as I know, there aren't any shortcuts. There is a guy I know who's been setting type practically since Gutenberg. He's as knowledgeable as anyone about the layout and style of print the newspapers in the state use. I'll ask him to take a look at the clipping, but frankly I don't think there's any chance he'll recognize it. Have you any idea how many newspapers are published in California?"

Paige shook her head.

"I'll tell you then," said Matt. "There are over a hundred dailies, and if you include every weekly, biweekly, and triweekly, the total must be close to a thousand."

"What if the search were confined to the area nearest Sonora?" she asked hopefully. "Maybe within a two-hour drive?"

For a few moments, Matt didn't answer. He drummed his fingers on the edge of the table as he mulled over this possibility.

"Even if you narrowed the area down," he replied slowly, "say to a hundred mile radius of Sonora—you're still talking about an area from Sacramento to Fresno, from Oakland to the Nevada border, and everything in between."

Staggered by the size of the undertaking, Paige said faintly, "There must be hundreds of towns..."

"Exactly. And if it were humanly possible to check with all of the papers in all of the towns, chances are it would turn out to be a wild goose chase. You don't know for sure that there's any connection between the clipping and our baby."

This time Paige was encouraged by Matt's reference to the baby as theirs. She clung to that and ignored the rest of his argument as she countered, "Except that Aunt Rachel kept it."

Matt glanced at the clipping and shrugged. "Maybe she kept it for the recipe on the other side."

"But, Matt, the recipe's incomplete."

He picked up the clipping and studied it again. "So it is," he acceded. "But the way the paper's torn at the bottom, it might have been complete when your aunt cut it out of the paper."

Matt's glance shifted from the clipping to her. His eyes were wintry and he seemed more distant than ever. He seemed unreachable.

"You've decided not to help me," she said dejectedly.

"I haven't decided anything yet, Irish. I want to

think about it before I come to any decision. Is there anything else I should know?"

"Just that I intend to go on with this, with or without your help. I have to know the truth." She extended her hands toward him with the palms turned upward in unconscious supplication. "If you do agree to help me, I can't tell you how grateful I'll be."

Matt muttered something beneath his breath. His tone was so low that Paige couldn't make out the words, but it sounded suspiciously like, "For whatever that's worth."

She recoiled as if he'd slapped her. Her hands fell limply into her lap and her shoulders drooped defeatedly. Although she averted her face, she was aware that Matt had gotten to his feet, but when he stood beside her and gently touched her cheek, she started.

She looked up at him, her eyes pleading mutely for understanding. His eyes were unfathomable.

"I'm going for a walk on the beach while I consider this. Do you want me to drive you back to your motel first, or would you rather wait here?"

In a small, wispy voice, she replied, "If it's all the same to you, I'd rather wait here."

"It may be a while."

"Even so..."

Matt nodded. For a few seconds more his hand lingered on her cheek. Then he turned and left the kitchen. A moment later, Paige heard the front door close as he left the house.

Chapter Eight

It's in the lap of the gods, thought Paige. She had done everything she possibly could to convince Matt to help her in her search.

It had been less than an hour since he'd gone out to the beach, but it seemed like an eternity. The hands on the wall clock in the kitchen moved so slowly that they seemed to be standing still, shackled together in an interminable embrace at ten minutes past two.

She cleared the table, rinsed the dishes and stacked them in the dishwasher. Then, because it was very late and she was extremely sleepy, she made a pot of coffee and drank two cups of the strong, bitter brew. After that she went into the living room.

She sat on the sofa, her head resting against the back. She felt completely drained.

After a bit she kicked her shoes off, tucked her feet underneath her, and curled up in one corner of the sofa, relaxing against the cushions. Her gaze wandered around the room as she fought to stay awake, and once again she was struck by the contrast between the elegant understatement of this room and Matt's old studio apartment.

Paige recalled the first time they'd met for a tutoring session. She hadn't yet tumbled to the fact that Matt was indifferent to his surroundings, and she had been appalled when she'd seen how cluttered his apartment was—or as he'd termed it, "lived in."

In the wall units of the studio, Matt's high school and college athletic trophies had jockeyed for space with rocks and seashells and a collection of beer steins. There had been several pieces of Mexican pottery that were quite handsome, and those had been transferred to this house. But there were also some items that were apparently prizes he'd won in a shooting gallery or some other carnival game.

There had been a few sculptures that looked pre-Columbian, several wood carvings she'd thought might be replicas of ancient fertility goddesses, and there was one object that she'd been very much afraid was a phallus symbol, but she hadn't wanted to look at it long enough to be sure.

Toward the end of the semester, when she had been more at ease with Matt, she'd asked him about it, and he'd laughed and told her it was only a cactus that he'd forgotten to water. He'd also made some wisecracks about obscenity being in the mind of the beholder, and how a girl as bright as she was supposed to be should know there was no such thing as an X-rated cactus.

But on that first day, she'd tried to ignore the item that had looked so sinful but turned out to be so innocent.

She had helped Matt clear stacks of records and magazines off the chairs so they'd have somewhere to sit. Their work table was buried beneath more magazines, his typewriter, a veritable blizzard of crumpled wads of paper, and the parts of a disassembled radio, which Matt had simply swept to one side and left in a jumble of speakers and transistors and wires.

At the age of eighteen Paige had believed her Aunt Rachel's propaganda to the effect that it was impossible to have an orderly mind if one were in the midst of disorder, and she was amazed by how much she'd learned when the two-hour study session was over.

As he'd rummaged through the cupboards at either side of the sink, Matt had said, "If I can find a clean cup, I'll give you some coffee before I take you back to your dorm."

"I don't really want any coffee," she replied.

"Not even if I wash a cup for you?"

She had tried not to stare at the mountain of dirty dishes on the counter, but it was obvious that she was dumbfounded. She had never known anyone who was as unabashedly untidy as he was.

At last, she'd blurted, "You have all the finer instincts of a packrat!"

But Matt had only grinned good-naturedly and retorted, "Now you know why my mother kicked me out of the house."

Smiling drowsily at this recollection, Paige eased her cramped legs from underneath her and stretched out so that she was lying on her side with her head pillowed on the arm of the sofa. Her eyelids drifted shut, and as soon as they closed she fell into a light slumber.

She was deeply asleep when Matt returned. When he lay down beside her and cradled her in his arms, she thought it was nothing more than a beautiful dream. He kissed her, and without waking up, she gave herself over to the taste of his kiss and the hard demand of his body against hers.

She pressed closer to him and opened her mouth, welcoming the sweet invasion of his tongue and responding unrestrainedly to it, returning each subtle movement of his lips and every dizzying thrust of his tongue with one of her own until neither of them knew who was the victor and who the vanquished.

When Matt ended the kiss she made a small sound of protest and her eyelids fluttered open, but even then the whole thing seemed like a fantasy, for he had only transferred his attentions to other parts of her. His mouth skimmed over her cheek, igniting a new fire when it lingered at the sensitive little spot behind her earlobe.

How many times had she dreamed that Matt was holding her this way? Kissing her this way? Touching her this way? How many times had she dreamed that his lips were caressing the side of her neck precisely as they were now?

He paused to savor the softly pulsing hollows at the base of her throat and nibble delicately at her collarbone while his hands solved the riddle of the fastening that secured her dress. He freed her of its unwanted restrictions, and when his lips resumed their downward course and arrived at her breasts, when his hands slid beneath her to remove her bra, she knew why she had chosen to wear this dress, because she was ready for him.

Her breasts seemed to spring to life at the touch of his lips. Her nipples were swollen, as ripe and enticing as forbidden fruit. He could not resist sampling them. But even as his mouth took possession of the trophy it sought, he was pursuing a new prize.

His hands joined in the sensual campaign, embarking on the journey his lips had charted, caressing her back and the curve of her hips, gliding hotly over her stomach. The elastic waistbands of her petticoat and pantyhose were no barricade at all. His marauding hands tunneled under both garments smoothly, unerringly, to claim the prize. He teased and fondled her moist, tender flesh, kindling desires that only he could satisfy. Instinctively, she raised her hips off the sofa, arching into his touch, and when he knew the prize was his, he probed more deeply, plundering the very core of her desires.

Paige wasn't fully cognizant that this wasn't a dream until the soft, mewing sounds she was making awakened her. Still half-asleep, she wrapped her arms around Matt, urging him even nearer, and when he resisted, she sighed, "I love you, Matt. Oh, my darling, it's been so long."

She felt him tense and in the next instant he had levered himself away from her and off the sofa. His stride was purposeful as he stalked to the window wall.

Devastated, empty, aching for completion, Paige pulled herself to a sitting position, clutching her dress about her.

Matt had opened the drapes. He was standing with his back to her, looking out at the early morning sky, but she could feel the hostility emanating from him.

Hastily, without bothering to recover her bra, she straightened her dress and fastened it. She located her shoes, and when she had slipped them on she felt a little better prepared to cope with the situation.

She couldn't bear contemplating why Matt had made love to her that way, *why he had stopped.* Not now, at any rate. She sat on the sofa, waiting for him to say something—anything.

When the silence lengthened, she stirred nervously against the upholstery of the sofa. "For some reason, I feel like I did when I was a schoolgirl and I was called into the principal's office without warning. Am I about to be reprimanded for some offense I've unwittingly committed?"

Unexpectedly, his tone deceptively bland, Matt asked, "How old are you, Paige? Twenty-six?"

Surprised by his use of her given name, she responded without thinking, "Almost twenty-seven."

She could have bitten her tongue for saying something so childish when Matt commented mockingly, "Twenty-six and a half, then. Surely that's old enough to be past the stage of innocent wrongdoing. You're not a schoolgirl any longer, and I think you're completely aware of all your crimes and the likely repercussions. In short, I suspect it's guilt you feel, plain and simple."

"Guilt?" she repeated numbly, bewildered by his summation of her character. "Why should I feel guilty?"

Matt turned away from the windows to give Paige a scoffing glance, and it was very nearly his undoing. Her face was cameo-pale, but her blue-green eyes were unnaturally bright, as limpid and clear as if a light were shining through them from behind. She looked so wounded, so vulnerable, it required a monumental effort not to rush to her side, take her in his arms, and comfort her.

How was it possible, he asked himself, that a woman who looked so innocent could be perfidious?

It's an act, the skeptic in him insisted. *After what she's done, you must know that it's all an act.*

At the skeptic's urging, Matt steeled himself to resist Paige, purposely whipping up his anger until it overshadowed his own culpability, until any lingering feelings of compassion he might have had for her were caught up in the white-hot maelstrom of his fury.

Yet he was more than furious. Paige's betrayal of him had shattered the last of his illusions about her. He bitterly resented that, and—yes, damn it!—his pride was hurt.

And, Lord help him, in spite of this, he wanted her.

When he'd come in from the beach and found her sleeping on the sofa, he hadn't been able to resist the temptation to kiss her. He'd thought he could stop with just one kiss, but when he'd taken her in his arms, when he'd felt the sweet weight of her against him, things had rapidly gotten out of hand. She was all silky warmth and soft fragrance, and he'd felt he would explode if he couldn't have her.

Just thinking of the way she had responded to him,

thinking of how it would feel to be inside her, to immerse himself in her softness, was enough to revive his passion.

But she'd been asleep. She hadn't even known who he was.

If he hadn't wondered whether she was always so generous with her favors, if he hadn't been eaten up with jealousy at the thought of Paige making love with another man, or if she hadn't lied again, if she hadn't tried to con him into believing she loved him, he would have taken her then and there. And that he had come so close to losing control of the situation added to his outrage.

Oh, he meant to have Paige, all right. If she was even half as anxious to learn the truth about the baby as she seemed to be, he *would* have her. But on his terms.

Why should I feel guilty? she'd asked.

Her question deserved an answer, and he was more than willing to give her one.

"Because you used me," he said abrasively.

"Used you—?"

He silenced Paige's objection with an imperious wave of his hand. "Hear me out," he said without inflection. He seated himself in the chair opposite the sofa, lounging into it so that he was half-reclining with his long legs sprawled out in front of him before he went on.

"Earlier—out there on the beach—some of the things that happened eight years ago began to fall into place. The way I figure it, you got pregnant as an excuse to drop out of school. I'm not saying you did it consciously, but that's what it all adds up to. That's why I say you used me. You needed a father for your child, and I was elected.''

"That's just not true, Matt! I loved you then. I love you now—"

"You *wanted* me then. You wanted to give sex a try the same way you wanted to experience any number of other things that were new to you, and I happened to be available. You *want* me now. I've just finished proving that, so don't try to deny it. Maybe you've got a yen to have another baby, but I'll be damned if I'm going to be your stud this time around.''

"How can you say that?" Paige protested heatedly. "You know perfectly well that if I wanted to get pregnant there are ways of accomplishing it without going to bed with a man. If I wanted to have another baby, all I'd have to do is pay a few visits to my gynecologist—''

"But that would be so clinical, wouldn't it?" Matt cut in. "For a woman who's sworn off test tubes and laboratories because she wants to be involved with people, resorting to artificial insemination wouldn't be much fun at all. Certainly it wouldn't be nearly as exciting as having an affair.''

"And if that were true, why would I choose you?"

"How should I know?" Matt replied disparagingly. "Maybe you're simply playing the law of averages. Lord knows I got you pregnant easily enough before. Or maybe you want the satisfaction of knowing you can entice me into taking a little stroll down memory lane whenever the mood strikes you.''

Drawing the tattered shreds of her dignity about

her, Paige got to her feet. She was trembling all over. Even her legs were shaking as she stumbled toward the hall.

"If you really believe that," she murmured huskily, "I guess there's nothing more to be said."

She was so horrified by Matt's accusations that she wanted only to escape, but he caught hold of her wrist as she passed his chair. She saw a gleam of triumph in his eyes as he pulled her between his legs and down into his lap. His arms locked about her, imprisoning her in a steely embrace, and his mouth descended to catch the fleshy part of her earlobe between his teeth and nip at it gently.

"Not so fast, Paige," he whispered silkily. "I didn't say you can't persuade me to help you. Who knows? If you play your cards right, I might be putty in your hands."

She struggled to break his grip on her, but he subdued her easily, half-turning her so that their legs entwined and she was pinned beneath him as they lay in the chair. Not satisfied with this, Matt molded her hips to his, grinding against her in a slow, circular motion so that she was keenly aware of the passionate surge of his arousal.

Her heart was racing, fluttering against his hand. She was panting for breath, more confused than ever as she stared up into the cold fire of his eyes.

"Wha-what are you suggesting?" she whispered brokenly.

"I'm not making a suggestion, I'm imposing a condition."

"A condition?"

Thrusting her roughly away from him, Matt sprang to his feet, leaving her huddled in the chair.

"I'll help you," he said harshly, "but only if you marry me."

"Marry you!"

He smiled down at her insolently. "There seems to be an echo in this room."

"Wh-why would you insist on marriage?"

"Think about it," he instructed her grimly. "Try to see things from my point of view. If there's a chance in a million our daughter is alive, and if she hasn't been adopted, I don't want to find her only to have you shut me out of her life."

"But I wouldn't do that!"

"Wouldn't you?" Matt's voice was heavy with irony. "You've already demonstrated your preference for keeping my child from me. Our marriage will be my insurance that you don't do it again. So my question is, do you want my help? Do you need it enough to marry me?"

Paige wanted nothing more than to bury her head in her arms and weep, but she gritted her teeth and refused to permit herself this indulgence.

"Yes!" she gasped. "Yes, I do!"

Wondering why he should derive so little satisfaction from Paige's capitulation to his terms, Matt pivoted briskly away from her.

"Very well," he said coldly. "I'll take care of the arrangements."

Chapter Nine

"I'd like to keep the clipping if I may," said Matt when he dropped Paige at her motel later that morning. "I want to ask Harve Jessup to take a look at it."

"Is he the printer you mentioned last night?" Paige inquired.

Matt nodded. "I'll call when I have anything definite to report."

He drove away, abandoning Paige to the torment of her thoughts. She was impotently enraged because Matt had intentionally set out to humiliate her. This time it was he who had seized the advantage when her defenses were down. He'd made love to her until her longing for him had reached a fever pitch, then he had rejected her.

But as angry as she was at Matt, she was even angrier with herself for allowing him to make a fool of her. She had sensed he could be ruthless. She should have acted accordingly. Instead, she'd made it easy for him to get the upper hand.

Paige passed the day in her motel room, waiting for the phone to ring and restlessly pacing off her anger.

By mid-afternoon the waiting had become intolerable, but at least her anger had spent itself.

It seemed unreal that with only the slightest token of resistance she'd given in to Matt's demand that she marry him before he would agree to help her in her search for the truth about their baby. In the hours since he'd left her, she had wracked her brain, trying to think of some way of proceeding without Matt's assistance, but there was no denying how desperately she needed his help.

Matt was aware of it too. And after the wanton way she had responded to his lovemaking, he must be aware of her emotional investment in him as well. Although he'd denied it, he must know that she was still in love with him.

Admittedly there was much more at stake now than there had been eight years ago, and even then it had taken every particle of strength at her disposal to decline his proposal of marriage. Only by tenaciously clinging to the lifeline of her pride had she managed to tell Matt that, much as she longed to be with him, she loved him too deeply to watch him sacrifice his way of life for her.

At eighteen, this response had seemed only logical, but at twenty-six, she recognized how melodramatic it must have sounded.

Matt had thought it was overblown, too. "The only part of that sentiment I believe," he'd retorted sharply, "is that you don't want to marry me. I sure as hell don't believe it's your reluctance to mess up my life that's stopping you. At your age, Irish, no one's that unselfish!"

Paige subsided wearily into the armchair nearest the window overlooking the motel parking lot as she acknowledged that, in that instance, Matt had been entirely correct about her.

Her actions hadn't been prompted solely by her concern for his well-being. She'd known then, just as she knew now, that she couldn't bear Matt's looking upon her as nothing more than a responsibility—like a favor that must be repaid or a debt that must be honored. She'd had enough of that sort of one-sided relationship with her aunt.

That she had met her obligations to her niece without complaint was a source of tremendous pride to Rachel Cavanaugh. More than once, she'd told Paige, "Maybe I haven't accomplished much else with my life, but I've always done my duty by you."

To Paige, who would have been happy to exchange all of her aunt's attention to duty for a bit of honest affection, Rachel's boast had been an unpleasant reminder of how much her aunt had had to sacrifice for her sake.

Eight years ago it had been unthinkable to Paige to marry a man who would treat her in the same impersonal fashion. That, she had thought, would be like jumping from the frying pan into the fire. And much as she loved Matt, the passage of time had not made the idea any more palatable. Yet what alternative did she have?

As the afternoon waned Paige sat in her motel room, waiting for Matt to call. She didn't bother to turn on the lamps or draw the blinds, and she stared out at the twilight covered hills and watched the lights of Santa Barbara wink on, but in her mind's eye, she saw a brilliant December day when she was eighteen. She saw the morning after the night she'd spent with Matt; the morning when she'd said farewell to her adolescent dreams.

She shook her head pityingly as she recalled her acute attack of morning-after angst. She remembered that Matt and she had strolled across the carefully manicured grounds of the country club, not stopping until they'd reached the shore of the little lake that formed a hazard to the fifteenth green. She remembered that, despite his insistence that they needed to talk, Matt had been strangely uncommunicative.

When they'd reached the lakeshore, he'd leaned down to pick up a few small stones which he'd thrown, one by one, skipping them far out over the water as if he were engaged in some sort of contest with himself.

In retrospect Paige realized that he must have been wrestling with conflicting emotions, because even when the last of the stones was gone, he hadn't looked at her. He'd stood with his back to her, his hands jammed into his pants pockets, watching a flock of gulls that wheeled and cried raucously along the shore.

Because Matt was so unapproachable, she had begun watching the birds too, wondering at his fascination with them. The wind had been so strong that sometimes the gulls were imprisoned by it, hovering stationary in midair until they were freed by a thermal that propelled them upward or downward.

She'd found their quandary peculiarly depressing.

Poor seagulls, she'd thought, *I know just how you feel.*

She'd felt as if she too were struggling to overcome some powerful, invisible force, being buffeted about by Matt's indifference.

"I'm sorry about last night," Matt said at last. His back wasn't particularly revealing, but she knew from the stiltedness of his speech that the apology hadn't come easily. "Are you all right?"

"I'm fine," she answered with bogus cheerfulness. "There's nothing you need to feel sorry about on my account. I'm not sorry it happened." After a momentary pause, she added for good measure, "Actually, it's kind of a relief to have it over with—not to be a virgin anymore."

Matt started with surprise, but he still didn't turn around, and her mood became positively somber.

How can it be, she asked herself wistfully, *that we're like strangers after we've been so close?* She knew Matt's body as intimately as she knew her own, yet he was acting as if all they'd ever shared was the six feet of lakeshore that separated them.

"Would you consider marrying me?"

In the wake of her thoughts, Matt's question had come as a shock.

"You're asking that because of last night," she said faintly.

Her voice was so thready that it was quickly carried away by the wind. Matt had hardly been able to hear her. He was forced to move closer, and when he was within arms' length, he looked directly at her and replied, "I won't lie to you, Irish. It is partly because of last night."

Hoping he would not guess what it cost her, she responded brightly, "You needn't marry me, you know. Thank goodness we've made some progress since Victorian times. A girl isn't required to remain a maiden till her wedding night—not many people even expect it nowadays."

"What if you're pregnant? I didn't do anything to prevent conception last night, and I don't suppose you did either."

Until that moment, it hadn't entered her mind that she might have conceived, that at that very instant she might be carrying within her the embryo evidence of Matt's lovemaking. She turned away from Matt and spread her hands protectively over her abdomen.

"It should be safe enough," she equivocated. "Anyway, we can always cross that bridge if we come to it."

Matt had seen the instinctive movement of her hands. Evidently, he'd been touched by it. With his own hands on her shoulders, he'd spun her around to face him.

"I want you to marry me, Irish," he'd persisted.

He'd sounded sincere, and his face had been sober to the point of austerity, but Paige sensed that his determination was a mask for a more deeply felt ambivalence.

How many times had Matt made some casual remark that expressed his unwillingness to give up his freedom?

With this in mind, she'd tried her "unselfish" approach, and when that hadn't worked, she'd smiled at Matt as if she hadn't a care in the world and said,

"You've made a lot of wisecracks about how stultify-ing you'd find married life. Did it ever occur to you that you might have converted me to your way of thinking?"

Her flippancy might have been discordant, but that only made it seem more genuine. For a moment, Matt's face had displayed some indefinable emotion. Then, with a mechanical tilting of the corners of his mouth, he'd returned her smile. But his smile hadn't quite reached his eyes, and it was obvious that he hadn't expected her to use his own arguments against him.

"No," he'd said quietly. "I have to admit that never occurred to me."

"Well, think about it now, Matt," she'd returned. "This is the first time I've had any real freedom to do as I like, when I like. Maybe I don't want to give it up just yet. Maybe I'm not ready to settle for a steady diet of hamburger any more than you are."

After a long silence, Matt had replied with an air of finality, "Okay, Irish. You've convinced me."

Only as she sat in her room in the Dunes Motel, viewing her farewell to Matt with the greater maturity the last eight years had given her, did Paige realize that, convincing as it had been, her comment about a steady diet of hamburger had been an unfortunate gambit. Since it could be taken to imply that Matt's lovemaking had failed to live up to her expectations, the remark had a punishing cutting edge to it.

Was that how Matt had taken it?

After briefly considering this question, Paige de-cided that he must have.

No wonder his pride had been hurt! No wonder he'd asked whether it was marriage she'd objected to, or if it was he who'd turned her off.

She deeply regretted that he'd misunderstood her, because nothing could be further from the truth. Not only had his lovemaking fulfilled her expectations, it had surpassed them.

The truth was that before Matt's initiation of her had taught her differently, she had always believed one had to be experienced before one could respond uninhibitedly. She certainly hadn't expected to experience such intense pleasure—to experience rapture.

The truth was that even after all these years she could still be seduced just by the memory of the night they'd spent together, and in the final analysis, that was why she had agreed to his proposal. Because she wanted Matt; wanted to marry him.

It was as simple as that—and as complicated.

Chapter Ten

During the early hours of the evening, Paige willed the phone to ring, but after eight o'clock or so, she dreaded hearing its summons. She assumed that if Matt had learned anything conclusive from Harve Jessup he would have gotten in touch with her long before then, and when Matt finally telephoned, her assumption proved to be correct.

"Harve couldn't add anything about the clipping we didn't already know," said Matt. "Talking to him did serve a purpose, though. He confirmed that it would be almost impossible to find out which newspaper ran the article."

"What do we do now?" Paige asked dejectedly.

"Offhand I'd say our best bet would be to locate Stella Ackerman. Have you any fresh ideas how we might go about it?"

"No, Matt, I haven't."

"Me either. I'm working on it, but all I've managed to do so far is rule out certain approaches."

"Such as?"

"Well, it seemed to me we might find Stella

through her dogs or through the sale of her property in Tuolumne County, so I've been on the phone most of the day talking to various business and professional people in the Sonora area."

"And you didn't have any luck?"

"No, Irish, not much," said Matt. "I found the veterinarian Stella used and I talked to a number of people who were acquainted with her. She had quite a reputation as an instigator of protest movements. Evidently she lent her support to everything from preserving historic sites to trying to recall a Superior Court judge to spearheading a campaign to boycott a local feed store that she felt was violating consumer rights. To half the community she was a saint, and to the other half she was a thorn in the side, but it was always as a committee of one. From what I've been told, she never actually involved herself in organizations."

"No, she wouldn't have," said Paige. "Stella was definitely not a joiner."

"You can say that again!" Matt declared dryly. "I haven't found anyone who's been in touch with her since she left Sonora and I have only one lead."

"What's that?"

"It's not a what, it's a who—a guy by the name of Chester Moffett. Does the name sound familiar?"

"No. That is, I may have heard it when I was staying with Stella, but that's all. Who is he?"

"The man who handled the sale of Stella's kennel. I haven't been able to reach him yet, but his former partner told me Moffett had retired last year and moved to Solvang to be closer to his daughter and her family."

"Solvang!" Paige's voice was quavery with excitement. "Isn't that fairly near Santa Barbara?"

"It's about forty miles north of here. I thought the simplest way to check out Moffett would be to drive up there tomorrow."

"But, Matt, that's wonderful!" Paige jumped to her feet and began pacing to and fro, trailing the telephone cord behind her. "Why didn't you tell me sooner?"

"I didn't want to get your hopes up," Matt replied steadily. "Try to be realistic, Irish. Don't expect any miracles, because the odds are Chester Moffett won't know any more about Stella's whereabouts than anyone else I've talked to."

"He might know where she went just after she left Sonora though."

"Sure he might, but then again, he might not. And if he knows, that doesn't necessarily mean he'll tell me."

"Why do you say that?"

"His ex-partner gave me the impression that Moffett had left the firm under some sort of cloud. Apparently he was being investigated by the ethics committee of the state realty board—"

"I want to go to Solvang with you," said Paige.

Matt sighed with acceptance. From the eager way she'd interrupted him, he knew that his warning hadn't lowered her expectations. "I thought you would," he said. "I'll come by for you about eleven—"

"But that's so late! Can't we leave earlier?"

"I'm sure you'd like to leave right now, Irish, but

tomorrow's Sunday. If Moffett's a churchgoer, he probably won't be home before noon.''

When Paige had reluctantly conceded this point, Matt said, "See you in the morning then." As if he knew how slowly the night would pass for her, he added, "If you feel the need to do something constructive in the meantime, why don't you try to remember anything you haven't already told me about Stella.''

"What kind of things?''

"Anything," Matt emphasized. "Everything. No matter how unimportant it seems, the smallest detail could lead us to her.''

"I'll try, Matt," she promised fervently. "You can count on it.''

The following morning was the kind of blue and gold day that spring sometimes brings to the Pacific Coast. The air was balmy and fragrant with the scent of orange blossoms. Fickle April breezes rustled the palm fronds and blew billowy white clouds across the sky, throwing a patchwork dappling of sun and shadow over the landscape in a natural reflection of Paige's own indecision as she stood at the window of her room, watching Matt striding across the motel parking lot.

The previous night's telephone conversation had gone well enough, but after the unpleasant way their last meeting had ended, Paige was more than a little nervous about seeing him again. She wasn't sure what to say to him or how she should behave.

In a show of confidence that was far from real, she

threw a sweater around her shoulders and opened the door without waiting for him to knock. She offered him a tentative smile. They wished one another rather formal "good mornings," and as Matt escorted her to his car she was both surprised and relieved to see that he was not alone. There was another man seated in the back of the sedan.

When Matt had handed her into the car, he said, "Paige, I'd like to introduce Joe Hutchison—"

He got no further than this before Joe interjected, "Happy to meet you, Paige."

Grinning, Joe stuck one huge paw over the top of the bucket seat, caught her hand in his unconsciously powerful grip, and pumped it vigorously. Then he sobered and pressed her hand to his heart. His manner was almost courtly as he asked, "Where have you been all my life, pretty lady?"

Despite his roughness, Paige found herself liking this burly, ham-fisted man with the spaniel-brown eyes and irrepressible smile. He was as friendly as a puppy, and the open admiration she saw in his face boosted her spirits and worked wonders for her ego.

Matt glanced sharply at Paige as he settled himself behind the wheel. Her smile was wide and candid. She was obviously pleased with Joe's compliment, but he saw no evidence that she was flirting with Joe. There was no coyness in her expression.

Could he have been mistaken about her after all? he wondered. Was she as honest as she appeared to be? The other morning, he'd have staked his reputation that she was the most deceitful female he'd ever known, but now he wasn't so sure. In the interim, he'd acknowledged that his perception of her could have been clouded by his hurt pride. Time, he hoped, would tell.

Relaxing, he slammed the door on the driver's side and advised Joe, "Watch it, buddy. Don't get carried away. This pretty lady is spoken for."

"Oh?" said Joe. "By whom?"

"By me," Matt answered briskly. "Paige is the future Mrs. Jonas."

"Is she now?" Joe's eyes widened with amazement at Matt's announcement, then narrowed speculatively. "Does Cynthia know?"

"Not yet."

Matt bit the words out as sharply as needles. He spun the wheel and accelerated so that the car careened onto Cabrillo Boulevard with a shrill squeal of the tires that underscored his annoyance with Joe's question.

Wondering who Cynthia was, Paige smiled at Joe as she withdrew her hand from his and flexed her fingers to see if his bone-bruising grasp had done any permanent damage.

"Have you and Matt known each other long?" she asked.

"Not long," Joe replied, "but we know each other very well." At her inquiring glance, he explained, "We met about two years ago, in the mountains near the border between Afghanistan and Iraq. The hills in that vicinity were honeycombed with caves where some Afghan freedom-fighters were hiding out, and the whole area was being pasted by artillery fire. My jeep went off the road and caught fire, and Matt pulled me out of the wreck only a few seconds before the gas tank exploded."

Grinning, Joe punned, "I like to tell people that Matt kept me from going all to pieces, but the fact is, he saved my life—"

"And Joe saved mine," said Matt. "I was wounded by a piece of metal from the jeep, and he got both of us into one of the caves and treated the wound as neatly as a surgeon."

"Those were the days, eh, old buddy," Joe returned affably.

A doubtful glance at Joe told Paige he was only half joking. "You sound as if you mean that," she said hesitantly.

"I do," said Joe.

"But how can you recall an experience like that fondly? It must have been terrifying."

"I suppose it was between protracted periods of boredom, but there's nothing like a little good red-blooded terror for teaching a person what's really important in life—breathing, for instance!"

"I never thought I'd have to accuse Joe of being humble," said Matt, "but he'd gotten involved with organizing the refugee camps. He had a cause and he was deeply committed to it. Besides, once you've gone through a thing like that, you feel you can survive anything. It takes something catastrophic to faze you."

"That's for sure!" Joe agreed wholeheartedly. "There's something about staring death in the face that tends to bring out the best and the worst in people. To give you an idea what it was like, Matt and

I spent almost seventy-two hours in that stinking hell-hole, along with an Afghan guerrilla and his donkey. We were jammed into that cave like sardines in a can. It was hotter than the hinges of Hades during the day and colder than a harlot's heart at night. By the time the shelling stopped, I figured none of us had any secrets from the others.

"Matt and I had taught the Afghan to cuss in English, Spanish, and French, and he'd taught us how to deliver the ultimate insults in the three dialects he knew—Pushtu, Dari Persian, and Uzbek. And let me tell you, all of us learned a hell of a lot more about donkeys than anyone in their right mind would ever want to know! But just when I think I know everything there is to know about Matt, he tosses me another curveball." Chuckling, Joe finished, "I must say though, Paige, I wish all of his surprises were as gorgeously curvy as you."

This time Paige joined Joe in laughing at his pun, mostly because he enjoyed it so much.

"Thanks for the lovely compliment," she said. "You certainly do have a way with words."

"You noticed!" Joe exclaimed delightedly.

Giggling, she asked, "Are you a newspaperman too?"

"Yep," he replied. "These days Matt and I work out of the same office."

He immediately launched into another anecdote. This one was also larded with praise for her, and now that a precedent had been set, she repaid his compliment with another of her own. They continued trading accolades, each of them trying to top the other, while Matt seemed content to listen to them. He grinned now and then, like a proud father watching his offspring show off, and sometimes he grimaced at one of Joe's more atrocious puns.

Paige found Joe's company so amusing, she barely noticed that Matt had left the freeway for the road that led to the airport.

As he pulled into the drive that wound around the front of the terminal building, Matt said dryly, "If the two of you can tear yourselves away from the meeting of your mutual admiration society, I'd like to know where Joe wants me to drop him."

Smiling sheepishly, Joe replied, "Anywhere along here will be fine."

Matt pulled into the curb near the main entrance and Joe climbed out of the car.

"Thanks for the ride, Matt," he said. "Give me a call tonight if you decide you want that lift to Sonora."

"Will do," Matt agreed. "Have a good flight."

Joe acknowledged Matt's pleasantry with a wave of his hand and started away from the car. As the swinging door to the terminal closed behind him, he blew a kiss to Paige and called, "Hope to see you again soon, darlin'. It's been a rare pleasure."

She was still smiling when Matt turned the car toward the freeway. "Joe's very likable," she said.

"I'm glad you think so," said Matt. "You'll probably be seeing a lot of him."

"Where was he bound for?"

"Nowhere special. Joe pilots his own plane, and today he's going up just for the fun of it."

"And you're planning on flying to Sonora with him?"

Matt nodded. "If Chester Moffett can't help us, I thought I'd go up there. That way I can check the records of the sale of Stella's property at the courthouse and make some personal inquiries around the town."

"When would you go?"

"If it's necessary, tomorrow."

"Can I go with you?"

"Not this time, Irish," Matt answered gently. "I'd like to get the trip out of the way in one day, and Joe's Piper has room for only one passenger."

For a while they rode in silence, speeding through the softly rolling countryside. Paige was aware that Matt glanced at her occasionally, but she refused to let her own gaze stray in his direction.

She focused on the scenery. Spring had turned the hills a tender pastel green. The roadside was studded with flamboyant pampas grass and with the delicate gentian blossoms of lupine, while the fields were lavender-hazed with the flowers of red clover and starred with cheerful orange poppies.

At last they approached Buellton and Matt turned off El Camino Real, heading east. Now they drove along a secondary highway that was bordered by tall evergreens. Between the trees, Paige could see the white-fenced paddocks and lush pastures of the Thoroughbred stud farms for which this region was noted. There were signboards to notify the tourist and the racing fan that this was the home of Post-Time Farms or Danceaway Stud, and a few minutes later they reached the outskirts of Solvang.

Paige found that she was nervously pleating her skirt, and she clenched her hands tightly in her lap to stop their fiddling and tried to concentrate on the picturesque little town.

Solvang had been settled by Danish immigrants in the decade prior to World War I. With its windmills, neat half-timbered gift shops, and thatched roofs with storks by the chimneys, the town resembled a little bit of Denmark; so much so that it required only the smallest flight of fancy to imagine they were actually entering a foreign country.

The sidewalks were crowded with tourists, and the traffic was congested. The bumper-to-bumper line of cars moved at a snail's pace along Mission Drive. At one intersection the cars were brought almost to a standstill by the colorful horse-drawn trolley that bused visitors around the town.

Paige leaned forward in her seat, as if her eagerness to be on her way might infect the driver of the trolley and urge him to pick up speed.

Matt fished a slip of paper out of his shirt pocket and double-checked Chester Moffett's address. He turned left at the next corner, and within a few blocks they were traveling through a quieter residential district. Matt made another left turn and parked the car near the center of the block, in front of a white clapboard bungalow.

Paige opened her door and got out of the car without waiting for Matt to assist her. Just as she started along the sidewalk toward the front stoop, a man came out of the garage at the far end of the house.

The man was only a little taller than she, and he was

almost as broad as he was tall. Paige guessed that he must be in his fifties, but his face was so round and smooth—almost featureless, really—that he looked younger. His thinning mouse-brown hair was slicked straight back from the high dome of his forehead, exaggerating his moon-faced appearance.

When he saw Matt and her, the man smiled and came down the walk in their direction, meeting them midway to the front door. His smile was certainly jovial, and he seemed friendly enough, but when he refused to look at her directly, Paige decided there was something sly and vaguely furtive about him. She thought he had hard eyes.

"Can I help you?" he asked.

"We're looking for Chester Moffett," said Matt.

"You've found him," the man replied. He pulled a paint-stained handkerchief out of his hip pocket, and after he'd wiped his hands, he held one out to exchange a handshake with each of them as Matt introduced first himself and then Paige.

As Moffett led the way into the living room of the house, Matt said, "I spoke to your ex-business partner yesterday, and he told me where we might find you."

"You talked to Artie!" Moffett exclaimed excitedly. "How is the old son of a gun?"

"He sounded well, Mr. Moffett—"

"Mr. Moffett was my father," Moffett broke in. "Call me Chet."

"All right, Chet."

"Fair enough! Now, tell me, what did Artie have to say for himself?"

"He asked me to relay a message for him—said to tell you he'd finally unloaded the Conyers' place."

"If that's not the darndest news since Hector was a pup!" Moffett threw his head back and let out a hearty cackle of laughter. "I always knew old Artie could sell sand to the Arabs if he put his mind to it, but I never expected *anyone* to be able to sell that old house."

Mr. Moffett continued in this garrulous way, telling Matt about his former partner in the real estate firm. He went into great detail about some of his own more memorable sales, and before long it became apparent that he was thoroughly enjoying the attentive audience he'd found in Matt.

Initially Paige tried to appear interested. She followed the conversation with her eyes, looking from Matt to the older man and back again, depending on which of them was speaking. But after a while she grew weary of Chester Moffett's long-winded boasting about his exploits.

He went on and on about how he'd happened to go into partnership with "Artie."

"Artie came to me fresh out of the army," said Chester. "He told me he'd decided to approach me because it was his ambition to become the best salesman in the county, and he wanted to sign on with someone who knew what it was all about. 'Course I don't mind admitting I was quite a wheeler-dealer in my day, but Artie seemed to think I was some sort of tycoon!"

I wonder where Artie ever got that idea, Paige thought impatiently. All she really wanted to hear was whether

Chester had any information about Stella. She wondered why Matt was letting the man ramble on so. She wondered how Chester had contrived to earn a living as a salesman. She wouldn't have bought a glass of water from the man if she were dying of thirst in the desert.

Now that she had given up the pretense that she was listening, her thoughts strayed further afield. She found distraction in the way the sunlight coming through the window at Matt's side accentuated the strong bones of his face and angled across his chest and shoulders, striking reddish glints in the smattering of fine dark hair on his wrists.

She watched the way Matt's lips moved as he talked, and she remembered the way he'd kissed her. She watched the way he gestured with his hands to emphasize something he was saying, and she recalled the way those hands had caressed her. She saw the way the powerful muscles of his thighs strained against his pant legs, stretching the material taut, and something inside her seemed to melt and yearn for him.

With a start of recognition, she realized the dangers of yielding to her desire to go on looking at Matt. She forced herself to drag her eyes away from him, and tried to think of something else, something safe and neutral.

She began by studying the pattern of the finely crocheted antimacassars that were pinned to the backs of the sofa and chairs. She counted the floorboards and the ceiling tiles. She had been reduced to counting the tiny fleur-de-lis that were woven into the upholstery fabric on the platform rocker when finally she heard Matt say, "Artie mentioned that you'd handled the sale of Stella Ackerman's kennel."

Suddenly intent, Paige gripped the arms of her chair as she waited for Chester Moffett's reply.

"That's right," he said. "That was about six—no, seven years ago. But it didn't take any special skill to make that sale. Truth is, I was sorely tempted to buy the place myself. It was one of the sweetest deals I'd ever seen."

"In what respect?" asked Matt.

"Well, normally Stella was pretty hardheaded, but for some reason she had this bee in her bonnet that she wanted to leave Sonora. She was overanxious to sell, and when the corporation that bought her place made an offer that was well below market value, damned if Stella didn't accept it. She didn't even try to dicker with them. You understand, there was nothing shady about the transaction. It was more or less a matter of policy with the group that bought the place to start out with a low offer as a feeler. In this particular instance, their conservatism paid off, because they got the place for a song."

"Would you happen to know why Stella was so anxious to leave Sonora?"

"She didn't take me into her confidence, but she was getting on in years. If you ask me, the kennel had gotten to be too much for her to keep up with."

"Do you know where she went after the place sold?"

"She said she planned to take a vacation, then she

was going to settle near her cousin in Redding, but she didn't."

"How do you know she didn't?"

"'Cause her cousin told me so, that's why. We were old school friends. We used to get together to go duck hunting every fall...."

Chester lapsed into silence when Matt pulled a small notebook and a ballpoint pen out of his jacket pocket.

"What did you say the cousin's name was?" Matt inquired.

"I didn't."

A calculating glitter had come into Chester's eyes, and seeing it, Paige knew why Matt had handled the interview so cautiously. Chester scratched his head and stared at Matt for a full minute, but it was he who ended the war of wills. Under the force of Matt's resolve, his eyes shifted away from Matt's and he squirmed uncomfortably in his chair.

"It was Otto," he answered. "Otto Ackerman."

Matt flipped the notebook open and recorded this name. Without looking up, he asked, "Do you have Otto's current address?"

"Hell, no!" Again Chester's rusty cackle rang out. This time he laughed until he was gasping and red-faced and tears rolled down his cheeks. "I don't know why you're so all-fired nosy about my business, Matt, but if you're with the realty board or Internal Revenue and you plan on talking to Otto about me, the joke's on you. You're out of luck—about five years out of luck!"

Matt glanced up from the notebook and sat completely still, watching Chester calmly until his laughter had abated. Then he reached into the inside pocket of his jacket and withdrew a leather credit-card wallet.

"I'm not an investigator," he said. "I'm a reporter."

He extracted his press card from the wallet. When he handed the card to Chester Moffett, Paige caught a glimpse of a bill that was clipped to the back of it. She couldn't make out the denomination of the bill, but it must have been large enough to satisfy Chester. In spite of the greedy way he stuffed the money into his own pocket, he eyed Matt suspiciously, making a careful comparison of the photograph on the press card with Matt's face before he returned the identification.

"Now then, Chet," said Matt. "What did you mean when you said I'm out of luck if I hope to talk to Otto?"

"Otto's dead," Moffett answered pugnaciously.

"I see." Matt's even response gave away none of his feelings, and his face was as devoid of expression as his voice. He got to his feet, motioned to Paige, and started toward the door, saying, "Thanks for your time, Chet. I appreciate your answering my questions."

Chester's beetling eyebrows were drawn together in a truculent line as he followed them outside.

"Aren't you even going to tell me why you wanted to know all that about Stella and Otto?" he asked querulously.

"Sorry, Chet, but I'm not at liberty to say."

"Well, if you use my name in a story will you make sure it's spelled with two *f*'s and two *t*'s?"

Chester looked lonely standing on the front stoop watching after them as they climbed into the car.

Matt smiled grimly, but he seemed to sympathize with the man as he replied, "Sure thing, Chet."

Chapter Eleven

The day had lost much of its luster. Colored by Paige's bitter disappointment, the town was no longer as charming. The sky was not as blue nor the trees as green. Even the warmth of the sun seemed to have cooled.

Shivering, she pulled her sweater more closely around her shoulders. Matt had warned her not to expect too much. "Don't get your hopes up," he'd said. "Don't expect any miracles."

But she had expected miracles. And now she was overwhelmed by an unreasoning fear that if Matt knew how disheartened she was, he would refuse to go on with the search.

She tried to conceal her feelings. She went along with Matt's suggestion that they have lunch and do some sightseeing before driving back to Santa Barbara. She even managed to produce a semblance of a smile.

Because she sensed that Matt was studying her intently, Paige kept up the pretense all the while they were eating in the windmill room of the Danish Inn and afterward while they browsed through some of the gift shops.

The stores were crowded but everyone was unfailingly cheerful. Gradually she fell under the spell of the day and the holiday atmosphere of the town, and her mood became less strained.

Matt bought several souvenirs for her: a rose-scented candle shaped like a water lily, a lovely delft-blue crystal paperweight, and finally a balloon.

She laughed along with him when he tied the string of the balloon around her wrist, as if she were a child and might accidentally lose it. The balloons that floated in the sky above the rooftops testified to the many times this had happened.

By late afternoon, when they were returning to the car, the gaiety she'd been pretending had become genuine. It was impossible to remain downcast when the bright red balloon was bobbing along behind her.

They had paused to look in a store window they'd missed on their way to lunch when they saw a dark-haired toddler who was crying over the loss of her own balloon.

Paige's heart contracted painfully with the sudden impulse to give the child hers. She couldn't bear seeing the little girl's tears, and she glanced at Matt, silently requesting his approval.

"Sure, Irish," he said. "Go ahead."

Paige slipped the string off her wrist and looped it around the child's and as soon as the little girl felt the balloon tugging at her arm, her tears were replaced by a sunny smile.

As Paige watched the little girl run off to catch up

with her mother she thought that her daughter might
have reacted in just that way. A crushing wave of sad-
ness engulfed her, and she blinked back a sudden
rush of tears because her child had never had the
chance to learn to smile or run free in the sunlight or
play with a balloon.

But in the next moment awareness dawned, and
she dismissed her grief, telling herself fiercely, *No!
You don't know that. Your daughter might be alive.*

Then, forcing herself to smile, she exclaimed,
"Did you see the look on her face? She was absolutely delighted!"

"Yes, she was."

Matt was smiling too, but he'd spoken absently,
and when Paige turned to look at him, she saw that he
was scanning the throngs of people on the street. In
the next moment, he said, "Wait here," and began
dodging through the crowd, working his way toward
the balloonman.

Paige lost sight of Matt before he'd reached the
vendor, and when he re-entered her line of vision,
she was astonished to see that he'd purchased what
looked like the balloonman's entire stock. He gave
balloons to several children he passed, but when he
arrived at her side, he still had more than a dozen left.
Red and yellow, blue and green, they bloomed at the
end of their strings like comic flowers in a clown's
bouquet.

Matt had also attracted more than a few followers.
Children of all ages paraded along behind him and
formed a circle about Matt and Paige. A hush came
over the onlookers as Matt untangled one of the

strings and transferred it to his left hand, holding it lightly between his thumb and forefinger.

"Happiness can be as fragile as a balloon," Matt said softly. "And as elusive. Hold it too loosely, and it slips away...."

He let go of the single string he held with his left hand, and while the crowd was diverted by the balloon drifting upward, he separated another one from the cluster, grasping it so that it broke. Startled by the small explosion of sound, everyone looked at him again.

"Hold it too tightly and it breaks," said Matt. "And while there are times when the greatest happiness comes from giving pleasure to others, there are other times when it's best simply to let go."

With that, Matt opened his right hand. The crowd laughed, applauded, oohed and aahed at the spectacle as the balloons he'd released danced upward and were caught and carried away by the breeze.

Paige was as entranced as the others by the performance. She applauded Matt appreciatively, without recognizing the symbolism of his gesture. It was only when they were leaving the restaurant in Buellton where they had stopped for dinner that it occurred to her that Matt might have staged the whole theatrical display for her benefit.

Once this possibility occurred to her, however, she couldn't seem to stop thinking about it, and the more she brooded, the more convinced she became that releasing the balloons had been Matt's way of telling her to let go.

But let go of what? she wondered as they drove

through the darkness toward Santa Barbara. *Of my search? Of the past? Of him? Is Matt advising me to let go of all three?*

She didn't realize how preoccupied she'd been until Matt spotted the signboard.

"Damn it!" he groaned. "Why didn't I think of that sooner?"

"What is it?" she asked worriedly. "Is something wrong with the car?"

"The car's fine. It's just that there was a kennel back there. According to their sign, they sell standard poodles and Saint Bernards, but I was going too fast to make the turnoff."

"Can't we go back?"

Matt consulted his wristwatch. "We could," he allowed, "but at this hour of the night, it would probably be better not to drop in unannounced. I think we'd better phone ahead."

A few miles later he turned onto an exit ramp that took them to a rest area with a public telephone. Paige waited in the car while Matt made the call, which was over so quickly, she knew without his having to tell her that the people at the kennel were not acquainted with Stella Ackerman.

"I have some good news and some bad news," said Matt as he got behind the wheel. "Which do you want to hear first?"

"I think I already know the bad news," she replied. "They'd never heard of Stella."

"You got it, but the Dixons have been breeding Saints only for the last three years, so I suppose that's not surprising."

"And the good news?"

"Mrs. Dixon seemed to think that if anyone could help us locate Stella, it would be a professional handler by the name of Mitzi Vaughn. Unfortunately, Mrs. Dixon didn't have Mitzi's address or phone number. All she knew for sure is that Mitzi lives somewhere in the Los Angeles area, but she said Mitzi's so active in the dog world, she should be fairly easy to track down."

Matt hesitated briefly. He was obviously preparing to repeat his advice that she shouldn't get her hopes up, but when Paige limited her response to a single nod of her head, he realized the warning wasn't necessary.

She was thinking that with every fruitless lead they followed it seemed less likely that they would be able to trace Stella. And now, instead of finding one person, apparently Matt was proposing that they find two.

Matt started the engine and turned the car toward El Camino Real, and for the next quarter of an hour neither of them spoke. Paige didn't feel she could rely on hiding her emotions well enough to make the attempt at small talk. She felt like howling with frustration over their unproductive day.

"We're no further ahead now than we were this morning."

The sound of her voice fell like pebbles into the still pool of silence in the car, and much to her dismay she realized that she had uttered the complaint aloud.

"I wouldn't say that, Irish," Matt replied. "Every avenue we rule out is one less we have left to explore." He paused for a few seconds and she derived new cause for hope from his calmness even before he added, "I'm positive that I've heard that name somewhere."

"What name?"

"Mitzi Vaughn." He hammered the side of his fist against the steering wheel and muttered, "Damn, but I wish I could remember where."

Another long silence ensued. It was not until they were traveling along Cabrillo Boulevard, nearing her motel, that Matt spoke again.

"You've hardly said a word since we left Buellton," he observed quietly. "What are you thinking about?"

"Stella." Paige sighed. "I've tried and tried, Matt, and the only thing I've recalled about her isn't really new. It's connected with what you learned about her fondness for rabblerousing."

"Tell me about it," said Matt.

"Well, Stella was constantly writing very long letters—I guess, to be accurate, they were political tracts. At least, that's how I remember them. They dealt with every conceivable subject, and she'd send them off to newspapers and magazines and congressmen—anyone with any clout at all with the public. Anyway, she had quite a lengthy mailing list, and I spent a lot of time typing drafts and stuffing envelopes for her. Other than that, I can't seem to remember anything I haven't told you about her."

"Try not to worry about it, Irish," Matt said consolingly. "We probably have enough to go on right now."

Moments later they arrived at the Dunes. After he'd parked the car and turned the key in the ignition,

Matt yawned and stretched. Then he slouched over the wheel, rubbing his eyes with the heels of his hands. Paige's throat constricted with concern when she saw how tired he looked.

"Don't bother getting out," she offered hastily. "I can manage on my own."

"I'm well aware of that." Matt grinned crookedly. "You've always been Miss Independence. Just the same I prefer to see you safely to your door."

He pocketed the car keys and reached in front of her to open her door before he got out.

Paige collected the shopping bag containing her souvenirs. As she stepped out of the car into the starry crispness of the April dark, she asked, "Do you still plan on flying up to Sonora tomorrow?"

"Yes, I do," Matt replied easily. "It's a lucky break for me that Joe's going up that way, and I intend to take advantage of it."

"You'll let me know if you learn anything?"

"I'll call as soon as I get back," he promised.

With the coming of darkness, the temperature had plummeted, and Matt retrieved her sweater from the backseat and slipped it around her shoulders. His fingers brushed against the nape of her neck in the process, and although she felt branded by his touch, as if he'd left his fingerprints on her skin, she was grateful he'd remembered it.

She was grateful, too, for the steadiness of his hand at the small of her back as he ushered her toward her room. The warmth of his hand seeped through the material of her blouse, and she wished he might infuse her with his strength just as easily.

She dug her key out of the pocket of her sweater and handed it to Matt. After he'd unlocked the door for her, he turned to leave, but he'd taken only a step or two when he swiveled around to look at her. Since he was standing on the blacktop while she stood on the concrete step in front of her room, their eyes were nearly on the same level. By the light of the carriage lamp above her door, she could see that his eyes were shadowed with fatigue. His expression was faintly troubled.

"It's been seven years since Stella left Sonora, Irish. That's a long time."

Paige nodded. "I know it is, Matt, and I'll try not to expect any miracles."

She turned to go into her room, but Matt detained her, catching hold of her arm. Her eyes widened, unwittingly provocative, as she turned to face him.

"Did you want something else?" she asked.

"Only this," he whispered. He folded her in his arms and kissed her, sweetly and with affection rather than passion. His arms were warm and strong, a haven she felt she never wanted to leave.

It was Matt who ended the contact of their lips, cupping her shoulders and gently pushing her away from him before he could succumb to the desire to kiss her as deeply as he wanted to. His hands coasted smoothly along the slim, pale column of her neck to her face.

"Whenever I touch you, I'm surprised to find you're flesh and blood and not just a memory." He turned her head slightly from side to side between the hard warmth of his palms and looked at her searchingly.

Had he been wrong about her? Was she as guileless as she seemed? He'd watched her closely all day. He'd seen the deep sorrow beneath the tranquil surface she'd presented, but other than that, not once had he seen any evidence that she was anything but what she appeared to be.

The uneven quality of his voice revealed his bemusement as he said, "I wish I knew what's been going on inside that stubborn little mind of yours all evening."

"I haven't been thinking of anything that's terribly profound, Matt," she murmured. "It's only—only—"

"Only what?" Matt probed.

"Only that sometimes it's hard to let go.".

"Nobody ever said it was easy, Irish, especially when you're wound up as tight as a two-dollar watch trying to keep up that unruffled appearance of yours. But keep your chin up, lady." Matt brushed his knuckles against the point of her jaw. "You'll know when the time is right and when it is, you'll be able to do it."

Paige drew in her breath to ask Matt exactly what he meant by his cryptic reference to letting go, but before she could form the words, he placed a silencing finger on her parted lips. He turned and strode quickly away from her, his footsteps echoing dully against the macadam surface of the parking lot.

Leaning back against the door, Paige watched while he got into his car and drove away. She stared after the car long after it had turned the corner at Cabrillo Boulevard and disappeared.

She fervently wished that Matt had allowed her to ask her question, but was unaware that she had raised one hand to her mouth as though she might recreate the touch of Matt's lips on hers.

Chapter Twelve

It was Monday night before Matt got back from Sonora. When he hadn't called by mid-afternoon, Paige phoned his office. Between that first call at three o'clock and seven that evening, when she finally got to speak to Matt, she called so many times that by the end of the workday she was on a first-name basis with Judy Garcia, his secretary.

During their third conversation Paige requested that the secretary ask Matt to call her the minute he got in. Trying to stress the importance of her message, she added, "I'm terribly anxious to talk to him."

"You and half of Santa Barbara!" Judy snapped.

Wondering what she had done to warrant such an unprofessional reaction, Paige apologized stiffly, "I'm sorry if I've been a nuisance."

"Oh, Lord," Judy wailed. "I'm the one who's sorry. I know it's no excuse, but I'm never at my most tactful when I'm under pressure, and boy, have I been under pressure today. It's been one of those days when the phones have been driving me crazy.

You haven't been a nuisance at all, but Cynthia Waring has been calling every five minutes looking for Matt. And would she take my word that he's out of town? Oh, no! Not Cynthia. I really shouldn't complain about her because most of the time she goes overboard trying to be helpful, but today she's been doing her queen of diamonds routine. She even came by to snoop around the office, and she's been a royal pain in the you-know-what. With one thing and another, I haven't been able to get a lick of work done."

Paige was won over by Judy's plaintive frankness. Besides, although she hadn't met Cynthia Waring, she doubted that she'd like Cynthia any more than Judy did.

"I know how frustrating that can be," she sympathized, "and I'll try not to bother you again."

"Please, Paige, believe me when I say you haven't been a bother," Judy pleaded. "I've really been looking forward to meeting the woman who managed to corral the wily Matt Jonas!"

"He told you—"

"That you're getting married?" Judy broke in gleefully. "He sure as heck did!"

Somehow, hearing this from a third party made their impending wedding seem more real. Paige was mute with astonishment. She opened her mouth to reply, but when she couldn't make any words come out, Judy rushed to fill the conspicuous silence.

"I hope I haven't said anything I shouldn't have. Joe says he's amazed whenever he sees me walking because I'm constantly putting one foot in my mouth!"

"It's no secret, Judy," Paige answered almost inaudibly. "I guess I was just surprised that Matt had told you about our—er, our plans."

"Well, since I knew something was up as soon as Matt asked me to try and clear his calendar for next week, he pretty much had to tell me you're getting married Friday."

"Friday?" Paige repeated dazedly. "He told you that?"

My God, she thought. Friday was only a little more than three days away!

"Are you all right, Paige?" Judy jokingly inquired. "You sound almost as if you didn't know when your own wedding is going to be."

Hoping Judy would attribute her nearly panicky state to bridal jitters, Paige laughed shakily and hedged, "Is anyone ever completely all right the week before their wedding?"

She and Judy chatted a few minutes longer before they said good-bye, and she spent the next few hours desperately striving to quiet her emotional turmoil. At least, she thought ruefully, Judy had given her something new to think about while she waited for word from Matt.

That word, when it came, was that he'd found no new information in the documents that recorded the sale of Stella's property.

"The only address the register of deeds had was the one at Stella's kennel," Matt reported.

"So it was another blind alley," Paige grumbled. "What are you going to do now?"

She had spoken more crossly than she'd intended, and her sharpness strained Matt's patience to the breaking point.

"In a few minutes I'm going to have dinner," he gibed. "Then I'm going to bed. Barring fires, floods, earthquakes, and other major disasters, I hope, for once, to get a decent night's sleep."

Matt practically roared the last of his answer, and Paige was forced to hold the receiver some distance away from her ear until his sigh signaled the next topic on his agenda.

"Now about the wedding," he said. "I'd like to get the license first thing tomorrow—"

Quickly, in a no-nonsense way, Matt outlined his plans, and Paige was so ashamed of having given way to grouchiness that she agreed to them without quibbling over the details. After they'd arranged to meet at the courthouse at nine the next morning, neither of them was inclined to prolong their conversation. By then, Matt was so dispassionate, it seemed to Paige that there was nothing more to be said.

Matt's manner hadn't changed when they met at the county clerk's office the following day. But in spite of this, in spite of the pragmatic part of herself that chided her for being foolish, she went shopping for a wedding dress after Matt had departed for his office.

The sky was cloudy and the wind carried the scent of rain, but thinking it would help to fill the day, she decided to walk rather than drive from Anacapa Street to De la Guerra Plaza and the Spanish-style shopping arcade in El Paseo. She wandered through the colorful rabbit-warren of boutiques and gift-shops, window-shopping until she found a likely looking store.

But even when she was in the fitting room, wearing the dress she had chosen, the cynical inner voice continued to nag at her. At last she silenced it, muttering under her breath, "It's my wedding, and it's the only one I'm ever likely to have, so I'll do as I darned well please!"

The saleslady, who was kneeling on the fitting room floor, marking the hemline of the dress for alterations, looked up at Paige, alarmed.

"Is something wrong, miss?" she inquired.

"No," Paige hurriedly replied. "I was just thinking out loud."

The woman returned to her marking and pinning. "Did you say you're getting married?"

"That's right," Paige said diffidently. "This Friday."

"Well, you've certainly made a perfect choice in this dress. It's lovely the way it matches your eyes." After collecting her chalk and tape measure and pincushion, the saleslady got to her feet. "I'll just pin the waistline, then you'll be able to see how perfect it will be."

The dress was lovely, Paige acknowledged when the woman had finished and left her alone, discreetly giving her a few minutes of privacy to admire her selection in the three-way mirror.

Not only did the aquamarine crepe match her eyes, it brought out the red-gold highlights in her hair, while the bateau neckline revealed the delicate curve of her throat and shoulders, and the cummerbund emphasized the graceful contours of her figure. The dress made her look so romantic—so bridelike—that she was perilously close to tears when the saleslady returned to the cubicle to help her out of the garment.

"There, there, dear," the woman clucked soothingly. "You're going to be an absolutely beautiful bride."

But it wasn't being Matt's bride that made Paige feel like crying. What she found distressing was the prospect of being his wife.

As she left the boutique, she was thinking that if Matt loved her—even if only a fraction as much as she loved him—she would be blissfully happy.

The sun chose that moment to peek out from behind the clouds, and Paige's spirits lifted when she felt its warm caress on her cheek.

"Happy the bride the sun shines on." Wasn't that the way the old saying went? Perhaps she loved Matt enough to sustain both of them. She loved him so much that surely, someday, he would have to love her just a little in return.

Paige returned to her motel, but she received no further word from Matt that afternoon or evening. She grew increasingly restive when the communications blackout persisted into Wednesday morning, but her pride wouldn't let her phone him.

In the solitary confinement imposed by the four walls of her room, her misgivings about their marriage loomed larger and larger. By midday they had reached monumental proportions, and she decided she'd had enough of cooling her heels, waiting for the phone to ring.

The weather had cleared, and although she'd spoken disparagingly about Santa Barbara's subtropical climate, the sunshine, the balmy breeze, and the swaying palms beckoned her. She left her room, and once in her car, she drove away from the motel as eagerly as a child released from school for summer vacation.

She drove aimlessly at first, but when she spied a hobby shop on one of the side streets that ran into Cabrillo Boulevard, she swerved into the right-turn lane and circled back to the store.

Aside from the rough sketches she sometimes made in planning her more complicated window displays, she hadn't done any drawing since high school, but now she was reminded of how much she had enjoyed her art classes. She went into the shop and bought a sketch pad and an assortment of pastels and drawing pencils.

On returning to her car, she found the city map in the glove compartment. After debating which of the local tourist attractions would be least taxing to her limited artistic skills, she settled on the Mission Santa Barbara. Because of the classical symmetry of its twin-towered facade, it was so well-known that even she should be able to produce a recognizable facsimile with paper and pencil.

At the mission she treated herself to a self-guided tour and passed an enchanted hour or so viewing the Indian and Mexican art in the curio room before she sat down with her sketch pad in a sunlit corner of the garden.

What Paige lacked in talent, she made up for in enthusiasm. She was so engrossed with trying to sketch the mellow, ivory-walled, Spanish renaissance mission that the afternoon fairly flew by.

That night she slept soundly, dreamlessly, for the first time since she'd left Mill Valley, and she was up before the sun on Thursday morning, following the coastal roads north.

She stopped to watch the sunrise over the Santa Ynez Mountains, and a little later she stopped again to try to capture the otherworldly look of an oil field where the spare, steely skeletons of the rigs reminded her of mechanical birds pecking at the ground. In her drawing, the rigs looked like so many giant-sized chickens scratching in a barnyard.

When she reached a remote, rocky headland and parked the car in a turnout, she felt carefree, as if her humble sketches had provided a much needed emotional catharsis. She raced the wind across the dunes, scratching her ankles on the spiky tufts of beach grasses that grew there, and danced in and out of the waves for a time before she collected her pad, pastels, and pencils, and climbed to the very top of the highest of the promontories that vaulted from the sea along that stretch of coastline. Once there, she lost herself in her drawing.

She took a break for lunch when she could no longer ignore the rumblings of her stomach. Then, driving a few miles back the way she'd come, she went into a diner whose weather-beaten sign promised homemade clam chowder and apple pie "like Grandma used to make."

The meal the café served didn't live up to its advertisement, but Paige was too hungry to care. She ate heartily and left the diner to return to the beach.

Her step was light and quick with anticipation as she set off across the dunes for the second time that day. The tide was out, and she spent the next several hours walking along the hard-packed sand at the edge of the surf, filling the pockets of her jeans with shells and bits of driftwood and other flotsam the ocean had cast ashore, pausing only to observe the fragile aquatic life in the occasional tide pool she came upon.

The only other person she saw that afternoon was a horseback rider far in the distance. She lost track of time, but when the tide started to rise she moved closer to the road and resumed her drawing, sketching fast and furiously, as though she must record everything about this enchantingly desolate spot before the light began to fade.

She stayed on until the sun had gone down, and when it was too dark for her to make any more sketches, she worked her way back to the car.

She felt at peace with herself. She was contented and more than a little proud of the way she had kept her apprehensions about her fast-approaching marriage to Matthew from spoiling the tranquil interlude of the past two days.

She had to stop at the boutique in El Paseo to pick up her wedding dress, but that chore was accomplished so rapidly that she was still able to keep reality at bay when she arrived at the motel. She had barely had time to put away the sketch pad and hang the turquoise crepe dress in the closet, however, when someone pounded at her door.

From the impatience of the knocking, she knew it was Matt before she opened the door, but she was disconcerted when she discovered he was not alone. There was a young woman with him—the blonde from the photograph Paige had seen at his house, the "friend" who had served as Matt's interior decorator.

Was she Cynthia Waring, Judy Garcia's "queen of diamonds"? Paige thought that if she wasn't, she ought to be, because what looked like real diamonds sparkled at her throat and wrists. Furthermore, she was even more stunning in person than she had appeared in the picture.

She was wearing black suede knickers with a tunic of some silvery synthetic stuff that caught the light and glittered whenever she moved. The outfit was so high-fashion, it was obvious that it had to be several seasons ahead of its time, but the blond woman wore it with such panache that it seemed completely right for her. And she smelled as expensive as she looked, of some perfume Paige could not identify. But, Paige thought, if orchids had a fragrance, their scent must be precisely that glamorous hothouse blend of musk and spice.

By contrast with the stylishly dressed blonde, Paige felt even more grubby than she had before. Her jeans and sweater were embedded with sand, and she was keenly aware that she was sunburned and windblown. Her nose must be as red and shiny as a beacon, and her hair was every whichway, straggling out of its pigtails. She hadn't bothered to renew her makeup after lunch, so she knew she must have long since eaten off the last of the lipstick she'd applied that morning.

All the while Paige was engaged in making comparisons that were woefully unfavorable to herself, Matt was glaring at her angrily. When she finally noticed this, her dismay gave way to irritation that he'd put her in such an untenable position by bringing his elegant girlfriend with him on this unannounced visit, and she glared back at him.

"Where the hell have you been?" Matt demanded as he strode, uninvited, into the room. "I've been trying to reach you all day."

Before Paige could reply, the blonde laughed and said, "I'd say that's fairly obvious, darling. It's easy to see she's been to the beach."

She laughed again, a merry little trill of sound that was as musical as a breeze sighing through windchimes, but Paige heard a hint of nervousness in her laughter and realized that the blonde woman was as uneasy with the situation as she was.

Slipping a graceful, proprietary hand into the crook of Matt's arm, the woman prompted, "Matthew, aren't you going to introduce us?"

"Sorry about that." Matt looked as grumpy as he sounded, but his dour expression warmed to a smile when he glanced at his companion. "Cynthia Waring, this is Paige Cavanaugh." In what was apparently an afterthought, he added, "Cynthia is the interior designer who remodeled my house."

"I know," Paige said tonelessly. "I recognized her from her picture."

"And I recognized you from Matt's description," Cynthia countered smoothly.

Did Cynthia's comment mean that Matt had described her as if she habitually went around looking like a street urchin? Was that how he thought of her? Paige was momentarily at a loss for words. Then, thanks to her aunt's careful coaching, she remembered her manners.

After wiping her hand on the seat of her jeans, she hoped inconspicuously, she held it out to Cynthia, praying it was not as sorely in need of soap and water as the rest of her. When she saw that it was smudged with pastels and graphite, she let it fall back to her side.

Cynthia simply stood there and watched all of this without once offering to return the courtesy, openly amused by the awkwardness of Paige's gesture. But in this instance, Cynthia had carried her condescension too far; far enough that the last thing Paige wanted was for the other woman to see how effective her deliberate snub had been.

Gritting her teeth, she tried again.

"I'm happy to meet such a gifted designer," she said evenly. "I especially admire the way you managed to blend Matt's souvenirs into the decor of the living room. It's unique and very attractive."

"Why, thank you, Paige, but I'm afraid I can't take all the credit for the way Matt's house turned out." To emphasize this point, Cynthia hugged Matt's arm close to her breasts and added, "It was a labor of love, you see."

"That figures."

While Paige's disgruntled mumble had been unintelligible, Matt must have sensed her response was less than complimentary, because he chose that moment to ask Cynthia to give them a few minutes alone.

"There's something I have to discuss with Paige," he declared, "so if you don't mind waiting in the car—"

"Whatever you say, darling," Cynthia agreed sweetly.

With a last meltingly compliant look at Matt and a venomous glance at Paige, she left the motel unit.

"Now, Irish," Matt growled when the door had closed behind Cynthia. "It's time to face the music. Just where have you been all day?"

Shrugging, Paige replied, "Sightseeing."

"Sightseeing!" Judging by his aggrieved tone of voice, Matt couldn't have been more indignant if she'd confessed to sleeping with the Sixth Fleet. "By all that's holy, I swear you'll have me climbing the walls. I've been calling every half hour, worried out of my skull about where you could be and what you might be up to, and you've been sightseeing!"

"Well, how was I supposed to know you'd worry?"

Matt's anger seemed to blaze even higher at her question. He closed the gap between them with one long stride and his hands clamped around her upper arms in a punishing grip, shaking her a bit before his hold on her loosened.

"Come on, Irish! Haven't you any sense at all? You've got to know how unpredictable you are. I've never been certain exactly what the mercurial Miss Cavanaugh might take into her head to do next."

"If you were so blasted worried, why didn't you call me yesterday?"

Between clenched teeth, Matt retorted, "I had nothing to report yesterday."

"And today you have?" Paige inquired skeptically.

"Yes," Matt replied coolly. "I think I might be onto something. You recall I mentioned that Mitzi Vaughn's name was familiar...."

Paige nodded.

"Well, I remembered where I'd heard the name. Cynthia's mother has a Yorkshire terrier that was shown to its championship by Mitzi. It seems she used to live in Santa Barbara. At one time, she was president of the Santa Barbara Kennel Club—"

"What help is that?"

"Maybe none, but according to Cynthia, the fanciers of purebred dogs form a fairly tight little community. Everyone involved seems to know just about everyone else—"

"You told Cynthia about us?" Paige cut in accusingly.

"I told her we're being married tomorrow. Since we had a standing engagement to get together for—uh—dinner on Friday nights, I had to do that."

Paige bristled at this bit of information. Because of Matt's momentary hesitation, she thought she could guess what had been on the dessert menu for those intimate Friday night suppers.

"I also told Cynthia that we want to locate Stella Ackerman," Matt went on calmly. "We're invited to a cocktail party at the Warings'—that's where Cynthia and I are headed right now—and I thought you might want to join us. Cynthia's made sure that Mitzi is going to be there."

Suddenly sensing Matt's thinly disguised optimism over the possibility that Mitzi Vaughn might be able to help them, Paige found that she had been infected by his enthusiasm.

"Oh, Matt, of course I'd like to come." Her tension drained away and she glanced down at her clothes. "I'll have to change first. Can I meet you there?"

"There's no big rush. We can wait for you."

"I'd rather you didn't. It's going to take a while—at least half an hour." Recalling how alluring Cynthia looked, Paige hastily revised her estimate upward. "Maybe an hour."

For what seemed to be the first time, Matt noticed just how disheveled she was. His hands skimmed over her shoulders to fasten on her braids. Tugging at them gently, he tilted her face toward his.

"I guess I can't argue with that." He smiled and his eyes danced roguishly. "Whatever you've been up to today, you look as if you must have had a terrific time doing it."

"Oh, I did, Matt, I did! I found the most spectacular beach. I can't wait for you to see it. And I've been sketching—"

He gave her braids a playful tweak. "Have you decided Santa Barbara's not so bad after all?"

"It does have its virtues. Any place that has poinsettias growing outdoors and spiders so big that you try to avoid hitting one with your car when you see it crossing the road can't be all bad."

Matt laughed. "You must have seen one of our larger tarantulas."

Paige nodded earnestly. "It was huge!"

"I'm relieved to see the roses are back in your cheeks." His thumbs were stroking over her jaw in light, repetitive caresses. "I really was worried about you, Irish."

"I'm sorry you were concerned," Paige said softly. "You needn't have been."

"I can see that now. It's just—" Pausing, he smoothed the errant tendrils of hair that had escaped her braids away from her forehead. His eyes probed hers, and when he continued speaking, he sounded oddly hesitant. "Irish, I hope you aren't counting too heavily on our child being alive."

"I try not to, Matt," she replied breathlessly, "but I can't help hoping."

His face was so close to hers that his breath fanned her skin. She was spellbound by his nearness, by the clean, tangy scent of his aftershave, and she was captivated by the tenderness in his eyes.

In the next instant, Matt brushed her mouth with his. He touched the tip of his tongue to the soft pad of flesh at the center of her upper lip, and suddenly she was on fire, tingling with awareness of him.

"Ummm," he murmured against her mouth. "You taste like popcorn."

"It's the salt air—"

"It's delicious."

His lips trailed to the corner of her mouth and across her cheek to her ear. Her head was spinning and she went limp and boneless against him.

Groaning hoarsely, he wrapped his arms around her and crushed her close to the hard angles of his body.

His mouth covered hers hungrily now, and she abandoned herself to the erotic play of his lips, to the sweet ravishment of his tongue. His hands strayed over the curve of her hips and found their way beneath her sweater to caress the bare, satiny skin of her back. Deftly, he unhooked her bra, and she swayed against him provocatively as her breasts spilled into his waiting hands.

She wished he would go on kissing her this way, touching her this way, forever, but all too soon he ended the kiss, withdrawing slowly, as if he, too, would linger if he could.

As he refastened her bra, he asked thickly, "Are you ready for tomorrow?"

"Tomorrow?" Paige echoed blankly, so overwhelmed by sensation, so distracted by his compelling masculinity that she could think of nothing else.

"We have a date to get married. Remember?" Chuckling, Matt molded her even closer. "I'm ready...."

"Y-yes," she stammered, shaken by the double meaning of his statement. "I can tell you are."

"How about you?" he whispered.

He rubbed his cheek against hers and nuzzled her ear and she clung to him ecstatically. Her arms were linked around his shoulders and her fingertips were digging into the cloth of his dinner jacket so that she could distinguish the individual threads from which the fabric was woven.

"I'm ready too," she admitted shyly, unable to deny her desire for him, not wanting to deny it.

Satisfied with her admission, Matt put her slightly away from him and grinned down at her.

"Are you superstitious?" he asked.

"Not very."

"That's good. It doesn't seem fitting for the bride to drive herself to the church, so I'd planned to stop by for you a little before noon."

She stared at him incredulously. "We're getting married in a church?"

"Where else?"

"I thought—" Leaving her explanation unfinished, Paige smiled at Matt, elated because he hadn't arranged for a businesslike civil ceremony that could be squeezed in during his lunch hour. Shaking her head, she said, "Never mind, it's not important."

"How about tomorrow then? Shall I come by for you, or do you go along with the old taboo that forbids the groom seeing the bride before the ceremony?"

"No, I don't go along with it, and yes, I'd like you to pick me up."

"That's settled then." For a moment longer, Matt held her close in his arms. Then he sighed and said, "Cynthia's waiting and time's a-wastin'. I suppose I'd better be going."

Turning her away from him, he gave her a light swat on the bottom to propel her toward the shower.

"I'll leave the Warings' address on the desk. Promise you won't be too long?"

"I promise," Paige answered dazedly.

As she went into the bathroom, she felt as if she

were floating on a cloud—a shimmering pink cloud of love for him. Inwardly, she acknowledged that, under the influence of Matt's intoxicating assault on her senses, she would have walked off a cliff if he had asked her to.

Chapter Thirteen

Thanks to the directions Matt had left for her, Paige had no trouble finding the Waring house. Although she had been in Santa Barbara very briefly only twice before, she was acquainted with the reputation of the Hope Ranch district.

Even in a city that was justifiably famous for its expensive real estate, Hope Ranch was impressive for its exclusivity. As she drove down the gracious, tree-lined streets, Paige thought that there probably wasn't a home in the neighborhood that could be touched for less than seven figures, and when she arrived at Cynthia's address, she saw that the Waring house was no exception. On the contrary, the sprawling Regency-style house appeared to be more expensive than most.

Both the driveway and the street were packed with cars she assumed must belong to other guests, and she was relieved to find a parking space large enough to accommodate her Toyota fairly near the front door on the horseshoe drive. Her battered station wagon stood out like a sore thumb among the Mercedeses, Porsches, and DeLoreans, and she counted no less than four Rolls Royces on the short walk to the house.

She made it into the foyer without incident, but just inside the entry a politely officious security guard took her name and detained her when he was unable to find it on the guest list. With a sinking feeling, Paige realized that Cynthia must have neglected to add her name to the roster. Certain that the oversight had been intentional, Paige was resigned to flunking the guard's third degree. She was preparing to leave when a darkly handsome young man breezed into the foyer.

"Derek Christopher," he announced confidently.

After checking his list, the guard waved Derek through to the living room, but Derek loitered close by. He studied Paige openly, making no attempt to hide his eavesdropping, and when he'd assessed her dilemma, he slipped his arm around her waist and told the guard, "It's okay, Chickie. I'll vouch for the lady."

From the guard's expression, it was clear that her savior's recommendation was of questionable value at best, but since Derek's name was on the guest list, the guard permitted him to accompany her deeper into the interior of the house.

Paige had time for only fleeting glimpses of gleaming parquet floors, sparkling crystal chandeliers, and richly carved wood paneling as, guided by the sounds of revelry, Derek hurried her toward the back of the residence. Her impression of the expansive rooms on either side of the hallway was one of blue silk draperies, priceless carpets, and period furniture of white crushed-velvet and gilt.

All in all, she decided spitefully, the overformal pretentiousness of the rooms they passed reminded her more of a museum than of a private home.

Finally they came to a less formal glass-walled room that opened onto a conservatory. Putting a protective arm around her, Derek shielded her with his body as he worked his way through the crowd to a quieter part of the room. When they reached the freestanding fireplace, he snagged two glasses of champagne from a tray carried by a passing waiter and handed one to her.

Paige accepted the drink gratefully. She smiled at Derek over the rim of her glass as she took a revitalizing sip of the wine.

"Thanks," she said, "I needed that. And thanks for rescuing me from the law."

"Any time, doll. Saving damsels in distress is my specialty, but don't you think it's time you told me who I've had the pleasure of rescuing?"

"Paige Cavanaugh," she replied.

"No kidding?" Derek's swarthy face was enlivened by an engaging grin.

Puzzled by his reaction, she said, "That's my name."

Derek favored her with a dazzling display of blindingly white teeth. His dark eyes were warm with admiration as they traveled over her features. He was flirting with her, but he did it so openly that she found it innocent and flattering.

"Yeah, doll," he said. "I'm real glad for you, but what I want to know is, are you *somebody?*"

"Somebody?" Paige repeated with some bemusement. "I'm afraid I don't understand."

"Then you've got to be new to this scene," Derek said amiably. "What I mean is, do you have any connections in the movie industry? Are you an actress, or do you work in the production end? Maybe in casting?"

"No, I don't."

"Maybe you're related to someone who's high up in one of the studios. Are you someone's wife, or someone's daughter?"

When Paige shook her head, obviously mystified by his questions, Derek studied her soberly.

"I've got it!" he cried, smiling again. "You're sleeping with some bigwig."

"No, not that either."

His face fell with disappointment. "Well, who do you know in Hollywood?"

"No one, I'm afraid. I'm here at the invitation of a friend of Cynthia Waring."

"Bingo!" Derek cheered. "Then you must know Cynthia."

"I only met her today, so I don't really know her," said Paige. "I take it that you do, though."

"In a way," Derek replied evasively. After a significant pause, he said, "Aw, what the hell! The fact is, I guess I know Cynthia about as well as anyone knows her. We met winter before last when I first arrived in L.A. She and I were in the same dance class, and she volunteered to help me decorate my apartment. Her daddy happens to be Mr. Megabucks at Nova Productions, and she even got me work in the chorus of a movie they were making—*Bound for Paradise*. Maybe you've seen it?"

Paige shook her head.

"I should've known." Derek smiled wryly. "It was not what you'd call a box office smash. But to get back to Cyn and me, we had a few laughs and for a while we were close—at least, I thought we were. Then I made the mistake of getting serious, and she went on to new game. Oh, we parted as friends and all. I wasn't dumb enough to get sticky about it. That's why I'm here right now."

Derek frowned into his champagne as he concluded, "Cyn's not an easy person to figure, but from the way she tries to buy friendship, I think she's convinced no one could ever love her just for herself. It's like she's afraid of being used if she lets anyone get too close, so she gets her kicks from the chase. Once she's got another scalp to add to her collection, she loses interest in a hurry."

By now Derek's expression was so melancholy that Paige felt like taking him in her arms and consoling him. But then, with a start, he shook off his dejection, propped his elbow on the mantel, and regarded her inquisitively.

"You're sure you don't know anyone important?" he inquired.

"Positive."

"Then what's a nice kid like you doing here? Are you hoping to be discovered or something?" Without waiting for her to reply, Derek went on, "I've got it! I'll bet you're an autograph hound. I'll bet when you first saw me, you thought I was somebody famous."

"As a matter of fact—"

"C'mon," he coaxed brightly. "Fess up."

"Well..." she began indecisively. At last, because
it seemed to matter so much to Derek, she fibbed,
"You're right. I did think you must be famous."

"I hate to disappoint you, doll, but I'm not." His
face was fiercely determined as he confided, "All I
really am is plain old Al Pinola from Keokuk, Iowa.
But I'm also one hell of a dancer, and I'm looking for
my big break."

"I'm sure you'll get it," Paige remarked quietly.

"Yeah?" he said dubiously. "No bull?"

"Honestly."

Derek appeared to be surprised and touchingly
pleased by her confidence in him. "I hope you're
right," he said, "but it means I have to be dedicated.
It means I have to make the most of every opportunity. If there's one thing Cynthia taught me, it's that I
can't let anything or anyone stand in my way." He
smiled apologetically. "Right now what it means is
that I have to mix and mingle. Do you get my drift?"

"I understand," she replied softly. "And I wish
you luck."

"Thanks, kid." Before he left her, Derek surveyed
the room and said, "It should be good. I've never
seen so many celebrities under one roof."

It was only as Paige watched Derek gracefully weav-
ing his way through the crowd that she became aware
that his comment about the number of celebrities in
attendance was no exaggeration. She became aware of
something else, as well. She was being watched.

Hastily she scanned the crowd, stopping when she
spotted Matt. He was on the far side of the room,
talking with Cynthia and an older, outdoorsy-looking

woman, and although he wasn't looking at her just then, she felt that he had been. She thought she detected a hint of arrested movement in the arrogant tilt of his head, as if he had quickly glanced away to prevent her learning he'd been studying her.

She watched him for several minutes, trying to catch his eye, but he didn't glance in her direction. Nevertheless, the more she thought about it, the more positive she was that Matt had been observing her closely. That certainly explained why she'd had a vague, uneasy feeling that someone was staring at her all the while she'd been talking with Derek.

At the moment, though, Matt's attention appeared to be riveted upon the two women with him, and on Cynthia in particular. Even as Paige watched, the older woman took her leave and he smiled lazily at Cynthia while she pouted prettily up at him. He lifted her hand to his lips and kissed her fingertips, her palm, her inner wrist....

Paige forced herself to look away from Matt and Cynthia. The romantic scene they'd just re-enacted brought back memories of the long-ago evening when she'd seen Matt and Carole in the cafe, and she felt as if she were watching a rerun of a very old movie.

She drank the last of her champagne, set her empty glass on the mantel and tried to recapture her interest in celebrity counting, but it was no use. Of their own volition, her eyes sought out Matt again, and this time he returned her gaze.

The impact of his eyes upon her was like coming into contact with a live wire, sapping her strength and rendering her mindless. When he beckoned to her to join him, she responded automatically, moving away from the fireplace and walking through the crowd toward him. It was beyond her to resist.

She told herself the only thing that had any real significance for her was learning the outcome of Matt's conversation with Mitzi Vaughn, but she was unable to convince herself that this was true. Ever since her aunt's death, she'd had an inexplicable urge to get in touch with Matt; an urge that had grown with every passing day until, at last, blind instinct had overruled common sense and led her to this moment. Tormenting pangs of jealousy gnawed at her, compelling her to admit that if she hadn't given birth to Matt's child, she would have contacted him on some other pretext. That much was inevitable because she was irresistibly drawn to him. Whether he wanted her or not, she felt bound to him.

Paige's step faltered as she realized that, at some time in the last few days, her efforts to discover the truth about the baby had fallen to secondary importance. Matt had assumed top priority in her life.

When she was eighteen, she'd taken a single glance at him and in that instant her life had changed. She was older now. In some ways she was more sure of herself, and she was much more determined, but all her determination wasn't proof against Matt's rough magnetism.

If she were to find her child, if a kindly fate decreed that she should be able to acknowledge her daughter and raise her as her own, life would take on a new purpose, a new meaning. She would finally understand joy.

But without Matt, something vital, something ele-mental, would be lacking. And without his love, she could never feel truly fulfilled.

It was only when she heard Cynthia's fluting laughter coming from the chatting circle of guests she was passing that Paige realized the other woman had left Matt's side. She felt strangely disoriented as she approached him. It was as if, viewed from the devas-tating perspective of her need for him, the whole world had gone askew.

Finally, she confronted Matt, and he asked, "Who was the refugee from Muscle Beach?"

Although he was only a few inches away from her, his voice seemed to come from a great distance. She stared up at him wordlessly, and when a full minute had gone by without her responding, his face hardened.

"Don't tell me you've already forgotten him," Matt said mockingly.

Paige shook her head, trying to bring things back into focus. "Forgotten who?" she asked faintly.

"The guy you came in with. Who else?" Matt re-plied derisively. "But, come to think of it, maybe you have a dozen or more like him stashed away up and down the entire California coast."

Stung by his sharply barbed criticism, Paige lashed out, "Since you're the original Johnny-One-Night, you have no right to complain if I have men stashed away along the entire Pacific Coast!"

"All right," said Matt with frightening calm. "You've made your point, but now I'll tell you some-thing I do have a right to complain about. I'm getting damned fed up with your throwing the past up at me whenever we have a disagreement.''

''If you're so fed up with the past, maybe you should break in a new act!''

Scowling, Matt demanded, ''What the hell is that supposed to mean?''

''Surely you recall the hand-kissing routine you went through with Cynthia a few minutes ago.''

Without warning, Matt's hand shot out and caught hold of hers. A warm, intimate smile replaced his frown as he raised her hand to his lips.

''Do you mean this?'' he asked.

In a practiced repetition of the gesture she'd watched him perform with Cynthia, he brushed his mouth across her fingertips. He lingered over the palm, swirling slow feathery designs with the tip of his tongue, before his lips moved on to savor the delicate skin on the inside of her wrist.

When her initial surprise had passed, Paige jerked her hand away, catching him off guard with the unexpectedness of her movement.

Raising one eyebrow at her quizzically, Matt remarked, ''You're overreacting. I won't bite.''

''At least biting would have the virtue of originality,'' she retorted unwarily. ''Since I've seen you audition that touching little piece of business, it's lost its power to charm.''

''Why, Irish,'' he taunted. ''If I didn't know better, I'd say you were jealous.''

''That's absurd!'' she cried, but her actions belied her denial. For a moment, she stared up at him, her heart in her eyes. "It's only that I don't much like your confusing me with Cynthia."

Matt's eyes raked over her. His mouth turned down at the corners, expressing his disbelief.

"There's no danger of that," he said tersely.

As he spoke, Cynthia appeared at his shoulder, looking suspiciously satisfied to have found them quarreling. She smiled smugly at Paige and linked her arm with Matt's.

"Hello again, darling," she purred. "Is this a private fight, or can anyone join the fray?"

"We've finished," Paige conceded. "Matt just delivered the knockout blow." Although she tried, she was unable to tear her eyes away from Matt's.

"Don't be misled," said Matt. "You might not believe it to look at her, but pound for pound, Irish is quite a scrapper."

"Oh, I'd believe it," Cynthia countered haughtily. "Really, darling, who wouldn't if they'd seen her the way she looked earlier this evening?"

Her peal of laughter underscored her disdain for Paige, but when Matt didn't even look at Cynthia, much less join in her laughter, Cynthia seemed to realize that she had overplayed her hand. She snuggled closer to Matt, glanced at him uncertainly, and decided that a change of subject was in order.

"Have you told her yet?" she asked.

"No, I haven't," Matt replied curtly.

"Told me what?" Paige inquired.

"I was waiting for a little more privacy," Matt intervened, hoping to forestall Cynthia's reply, but she was silenced only temporarily.

"Honestly, Paige!" she exclaimed. "Can't you see how unreasonable it is of you to expect Matt to track down this friend of yours—what was her name? Oh, yes—Stella Ackerman. After all, as Mitzi Vaughn told Matt, there are several reputable breeders right here in Southern California who are quite capable of providing you with a very nice Saint Bernard puppy."

Encouraged by Paige's disheartened expression, Cynthia went on, "I must say, it's a mystery to me why anyone would ask for a puppy as a wedding gift in the first place. Only someone with a tediously unromantic soul could possibly do a thing like that!"

Only as she concluded did it dawn on Cynthia that Matt had relinquished his hold on Paige's eyes and was frowning at her repressively.

Choosing to retreat rather than stay and face Matt's disapproval, she said hastily, "Well, darlings, if the two of you will excuse me, I really must see to my other guests."

Paige stared after Cynthia as she left them. Even when the blond woman had been swallowed up by the crowd, she refused to meet Matt's eyes.

"I gather Mitzi Vaughn doesn't know where we can find Stella," she said.

"You gather correctly."

"That's quite a line you handed Cynthia about why you're so anxious to locate Stella. It must have required an award-winning performance to convince her it was the truth."

"Not at all," Matt said dryly. "Cynthia was more than willing to be taken in." He hesitated briefly, studying Paige's tightly controlled features. She was pale with the effort of maintaining her composure. "I'm sorry Cynthia didn't give me the chance to tell you myself."

Paige shrugged with bitter resignation. "What difference does it make? We wouldn't be any closer to finding Stella."

"Tonight hasn't been a total loss," Matt hastened to reassure her. "Mitzi did say she'd check with the local Saint Bernard breeders to see if one of them is acquainted with Stella."

"And if they aren't?"

"Then we'll have to come up with a new angle," Matt said evenly. "If Stella's still active in the dog world, there are several avenues we could pursue. The American Kennel Club, various breeder organizations, licensing agencies—and if those sources don't pan out, we can still place ads in the major magazines the breeders subscribe to."

By now, despite her valiant effort to hold back her tears, Paige was blinded by them. When Matt wrapped a consoling arm about her shoulders, she leaned against him gratefully.

"Hell, Irish!" he muttered softly. "We're not licked yet—not by a long shot. If all else fails, we can always offer a reward for information leading to Stella's whereabouts."

Having offered what hope he could, Matt led her out of the room and away from the hubbub of the party.

Chapter Fourteen

They were married shortly after noon the next day in a small adobe chapel with a terracotta roof. Joe Hutchison and Judy Garcia were their witnesses.

Earlier in the day Matt had phoned his mother to tell her of their intentions, and Eve Jonas sent Paige her love and best wishes.

"She was delighted to hear I'd succumbed to your charms," Matt told Paige as he drove her toward the chapel. "She said she's known you're a miracle worker from the first time she saw you."

"At the tea?" Paige was wide-eyed with surprise. "I was so embarrassed that day because I hadn't dressed up. I wished I could vanish in a puff of smoke, but your mother made me feel welcome. She's so kind."

"You might have been embarrassed, but that didn't stop you from challenging Doc."

"You heard about that?"

"Twice." Matt grinned broadly. "My mother's version, and Doc's version."

"I imagine Dr. Jonas's version is closer to my recollection of that day." Sighing, Paige admitted, "I must have looked more like a ragamuffin than a miracle worker. There are times when it seems that I'm destined to find myself in all sorts of trouble, just because of my clothes."

"I can think of a simple solution to that problem," Matt said laconically.

Blushing, Paige retorted, "I'm not going to ask what it is. For some reason, I get the distinct impression I'd find your solution much more embarrassing than the problem."

"Ah, well," Matt intoned sadly. "To each his own."

He couldn't miss seeing the flattering tinge of color his teasing had brought to her cheeks, and the rest of the drive was marked by her silence and his occasional chuckle.

After the ceremony, the wedding party had lunch at a charming little bistro in Montecito where Joe kept all of them entertained with his puns, most of which were more than a trifle risqué. Matt had ordered a magnum of champagne, and as the level of the sparkling wine remaining in the bottle decreased, Joe's quips became increasingly off-color. After one that just missed being vulgar, someone kicked Paige's ankle. She let out a small yelp of pain, and when she looked around the table she saw that Judy was pink-cheeked with chagrin.

"Sorry," Judy murmured. "That was intended for Joe."

They had a leisurely meal, and when the other two

had gone off together and she and Matt were alone, Paige asked, "Is Joe always so outrageous?"

"Not at all," Matt replied, completely serious. "He was on his good behavior today."

Since they had to stop by the motel so that Paige could pick up her car, it was nearly four o'clock before they finally arrived at Matt's house. She followed after him nervously when he showed her to the master bedroom. She conducted a hasty inventory of the furnishings, looking for signs of Cynthia Waring's involvement with the decoration of the house, and relaxed a bit when she found none. The stamp of Matt's personality was so strong that it overshadowed any traces of herself that Cynthia might have left behind.

Despite this, Paige hardly recognized herself when she caught a glimpse of her face in the mirror. She was white with tension, while her eyes had a feverish glitter.

She encountered Matt's eyes in the mirror and a warm rush of color washed into her face.

"If you'd like to change," he suggested, smiling knowingly, "there's time for a walk on the beach before dark."

Not trusting her voice, she nodded her agreement. Suddenly she was lightheaded. She felt as if she were drunk when, in fact, she'd had only two glasses of champagne at lunch. When Matt had left the room, her knees gave way and she collapsed onto the end of the bed, momentarily overcome by the strange dichotomy in her emotions.

Part of her was relieved that Matt seemed to be in no hurry to consummate their marriage, while another part—perhaps the major part—was disappointed.

He hadn't touched her since the ceremony—now that she thought of it, he'd only kissed her lightly then—and she had to admit that she resented the casual way he was treating her. And although she knew how ambivalent he was about marriage, she was also confused.

She knew the chemistry between them was as potent as it had always been. Just last night, when he'd teased her about being ready for today, his own arousal had been obvious. But, she argued inwardly, such physical responses were involuntary. And anyway, her concern over their sexual relationship was merely the tip of the iceberg.

Eight years ago, Matt had proposed to her because his sense of honor demanded it. A few short days ago, he had ruthlessly rejected her. Paige did not question his desire to insure his role in their daughter's life, but surely he could have safeguarded his position by some means less drastic than marriage.

Had he married her out of anger? Or to salve his injured pride because he felt she'd used him?

Paige twisted the wide gold band on her finger as she puzzled over this. Several minutes had gone by before it occurred to her that it actually didn't matter one way or the other why Matt had married her. What was important was that she loved him and that, more than anything, she wanted their marriage to succeed.

"That's an impossible dream as it is," she muttered, "but sitting around moping about it certainly isn't going to make it come true."

Getting purposefully to her feet, she hurried to change from the turquoise crepe dress into a pair of jeans and a soft velour pullover. While she was tying the laces of her sneakers, she decided that her hairstyle was much too elaborate for a walk on the beach. Except for a few strands that curled around her temples and the nape of her neck, it was piled high on her head. She removed the pins that secured it, found her brush in her overnight bag, and brushed at her curls until her hair fell smoothly to her shoulders. After that, all that remained for her to do before she could rejoin Matt was to tidy away her things.

She hung her wedding dress on her side of the walk-in closet and aligned the sling-back pumps she'd worn with the dress on the shoe rack just below it with more care than was necessary. She hadn't unpacked the rest of her things yet, and the dress looked lonely hanging all by itself on the rod across from Matt's suits and shirts and coats. It looked out of place and, somehow, vulnerable—as lonely and misplaced and vulnerable as she felt just now.

Squaring her shoulders resolutely, Paige scolded herself for indulging in self-pity. But as she let herself out of the bedroom, she was thinking, regretfully, that Matt hadn't even bothered to compliment her on her wedding dress.

When she joined him in the living room, however, he rectified this oversight.

Smiling at her approvingly, he lifted a strand of hair from her shoulder and twined it around his fingers as he said, "You looked lovely before, but I believe I prefer you this way. Now you look like the old Irish—the woman I remember."

She wondered if he was building her up only to let her down once again, but despite her reservations, his slow grin was wreaking havoc with her pulse rate. Her breath seemed to have lodged in her throat.

"The new Irish is me as well," she replied huskily.

"I realize that, and I look forward to getting to know her—intimately. It's just that the old Irish seemed more attainable."

With that cryptic remark, Matt went off to change clothes, and hoping to avoid another bout with her apprehensions, Paige wandered out to the deck to wait for him.

Because the deck was built on stilts, a story and a half above the top of the steeply sloping bluff, the view was as panoramic as she had envisioned it would be. As she stood by the railing, looking toward the ocean, she thought that if she had been asked to design her dream house, she couldn't have planned anything that was more to her liking than Matt's house. There were perhaps half a dozen other houses tucked away among the dunes, but none of them approached the perfection of this one.

She inhaled deeply, drawing the fragrant salt air deep into her lungs.

The Pacific was living up to its name today. The waves lapped gently at the shore, garnishing it with scalloped swags of seaweed.

A volleyball game was in progress five hundred yards or so down the beach, and now and again the voices of the players floated up to her as they shouted or groaned or traded insults. Farther down the beach, where the sandy bluffs gave way to sheer rocky cliffs, a few fishermen dotted the shore, standing knee deep in the surf, while offshore a fog bank blanketed the surface of the ocean.

The false horizon the ribbon of fog created gave the clear blue sky above it the same suspended appearance as the sky in a child's drawing. Paige was entranced with the way the sun was sinking into the fog, turning the sky iridescent, tinting it with pastels that glistened like the inside of an abalone shell.

Only a half-sun was left when Matt returned. Without speaking, he took her hand, and together they walked down the stairs and started along the beach.

They had nearly reached the volleyball players, still without speaking, before it struck Paige that the silence between them was not a truly companionable one. Although he continued to hold onto her hand, Matt seemed to be lost in thought. He seemed almost distant.

"Do you ever join in the volleyball game?" she ventured.

"Sometimes," he answered shortly.

"Do all these people live around here?" A wave of her hand took in the volleyball players, the fishermen, and one or two joggers who had recently come onto the beach.

"Not all of them," Matt replied. "The beach itself

is owned by the state. There's a stairway to the public parking lot just on the other side of those cliffs."

"How about fishing?"

He looked at her absently. "Pardon me?"

With stilted formality, she inquired, "Do you ever do any fishing hereabouts?"

He nodded. "It's pretty good along this stretch of shore."

Matt's answer had been responsive enough, but he seemed even more detached than before. Paige's steps slowed so that she was lagging behind him, and when he didn't seem to notice that she was no longer keeping pace with him, she slipped her hand out of his.

Scuffing her feet in the sand, she trudged along behind him a bit farther before she spied an interesting looking piece of driftwood and stopped. She leaned over and picked up the boomerang-shaped piece of wood, and on an impulse, after weighing it in her hand for a moment to test its balance, she hurled it as far as she could out into the surf.

Feeling better for having vented her temper in this way, she raced to catch up with Matt.

His long, effortless stride had carried him some distance away from her, and when he rounded the rocky cliffs and disappeared from view, she ran even faster.

She finally caught up with him near a huge pile of driftwood logs that had been cast up on the beach by some stormy tide. She was winded and she had a cramp in her side, so she'd had to slow down considerably, and she wouldn't have caught up to him then if he hadn't stopped to talk to one of the fishermen.

Only slightly relieved that the chase was at an end, Paige threw herself down on the still sun-warmed sand to wait for Matt. Reclining against one of the logs where she would be sheltered from the nippy ocean breeze, she tipped her head back and watched him, admiring the athletic grace of his body as he talked with the fisherman.

Matt was standing with his feet planted firmly and wide apart. His legs were braced, his hands were hooked into the back pockets of his jeans, and his head was held at an unconsciously arrogant angle so that his posture reflected a combination of pride, aggressiveness, and supreme self-confidence. And when a gust of wind molded his clothing to the power-ful length of his thighs, to the width of his rugged shoulders and the well-defined muscles of his back, he seemed to blend into the implacable cliffs just be-hind him and become a natural extension of them.

He also, thought Paige, radiated sexuality.

She looked away from him uneasily, disturbed by the turn her musings had taken. Her thoughts had traveled full circle, bringing her back to the indisputa-ble fact that this was her wedding night, and that she was being sadly neglected by her husband.

Paige was vaguely aware that the conversation be-tween Matt and the fisherman had ended, that they were bidding each other good-bye, but it was only when Matt's body blocked out the little sunlight that remained that she realized he was coming toward her. His shadow washed over her, and she shivered with the sudden chill she felt.

Matt smiled at her, but she looked away. She was

perturbed enough that she was determined to remain aloof. After all, she told herself, two could play that game.

It became evident that it was going to require all the strength at her disposal to follow this resolution when Matt dropped down on the sand nearby and remarked with surprising cheerfulness, "Kind of a cold evening for a sunbath, isn't it?"

"It's not so bad out of the wind," she replied. She concentrated very hard on the letters she was scratching in the sand with a stick and kept her face averted, but her voice expressed both her hurt and her uncertainty.

Matt reached out and stilled her hand with his. When she glanced up at him, he smiled again in a boyish way she knew was intended to be disarming.

"I've been thinking—"

"Oh?" she interrupted stiffly, her pretense at indifference forgotten. "Is that what you call it?"

"What would you call it?"

"Ignoring me." Her eyes slid away from his when her voice broke on the words, and she began gouging at the sand with her stick, poking at it furiously.

"Is that what it's seemed like to you?"

Paige was appalled to feel her chin start to quiver at Matt's softly voiced question. He'd sounded so sympathetic! But she didn't want his sympathy any more than she'd wanted his lack of attention. The tender curve of her mouth assumed a stubborn cast as she pressed her lips together, refusing to answer his question.

Matt sighed. "I suppose, from that response, the

answer is yes. And believe me, Irish, I understand why you're upset. I know I've been inattentive, but it's because I've been so preoccupied—"

"Is this going to be an apology?"

"Partly," Matt admitted after a momentary hesitation.

"It's entirely superfluous."

"And am I?" he asked curtly. "Am I superfluous also?"

"What do you mean?"

"There was a time when you said you loved me. There was a time you even showed it," he reminded her cruelly, his tone even and confident. "Do you still feel the same way?"

For a moment she was tempted to cry out, "Of course I do!" The words trembled on the tip of her tongue. Her lips parted to say them. But a small inner voice warned her to exercise caution.

Matt was so sure of himself. What was worse, he was so sure of her. He'd played upon her emotions as if they were a musical instrument. Less than a week ago he'd made her want him, made her confess she still loved him. Then he'd taken great pleasure in withholding himself from her. He'd manipulated her into marriage and proceeded to ignore her, and she was tired of being taken for granted.

Paige jumped to her feet and took a few running steps away from Matt before she recognized the futility of trying to avoid this confrontation. Even if she could run away from him, she couldn't run away from herself.

Matt had followed after her, and when she stopped,

he was so near that she could feel the solid warmth of his body at her back.

If he touches me, she thought, *I won't be able to bear it!*

"Aren't you going to answer me?" His breath stirred the hair at the crown of her head when he spoke, and his deep, softly modulated voice wove a silken web about her. She was poised for flight, yet she was afraid to move for fear of inadvertently brushing against him. And with every passing second her resolve to resist his blandishments was growing weaker.

Hastily, she equivocated, "There have been times when I've said and done any number of foolish things. Undoubtedly I'll do and say many more before I'm through. But I'm capable of learning from my mistakes."

"So am I," Matt declared firmly. "Irish, would you please turn around so I can see you properly?"

"No, I won't."

She had replied crossly, and when he chuckled she was so infuriated by his laughter that she whirled around to glower at him.

"That's a little better," he said.

His face reflected the glow of the setting sun, and all of its warmth. He was still smiling, but as his eyes traveled hungrily over her upturned face, his smile faded. He wrapped his hand about her wrist and lifted her hand to his lips. Then, catching the fleshy pad of one fingertip between his teeth, he nipped at it until she cried out in protest.

"Why are you *doing* this to me?" she wailed, and

his mouth immediately gentled to kiss the spot he'd hurt.

"That was to impress you with my originality and adaptability to constructive criticism." Matt laid her hand against his face and slowly, sensuously, rubbed his cheek against the palm. "But more than that, it was to prove to you that I know exactly who and what you are."

"Do you, Matt? Do you really?" Tears burned her eyelids. "I wish I could say the same about you. I wish I knew what you want of me."

"It's very simple, Irish. I don't expect to hear from Mitzi Vaughn till early next week, and heaven only knows if we'll be any closer to finding Stella when Mitzi does call, but in the meantime, I'd like you to forgive me for my lack of sympathy when you told me about the baby. I know it's no excuse, but I was hurt and angry. I was blinded by my stupid pride and I made a lot of false assumptions about you. Can you forgive me?"

"Of course I can," she answered without hesitation.

"There's more," he cautioned. "I'd also like us both to try to put the past behind us. I'd like us to forget the reasons we're together now. I'd like us to forget the way we've hurt each other. I'd like us just to...be together. Do you think that's possible?"

Somehow his hands had encircled her waist and he had drawn her into his arms. Her hands were spread with fast-weakening resistance against his chest, and even through the thickness of his sweater, she could feel his heart racing beneath her palm.

"Oh, Matt," she replied recklessly, "I don't know if it's possible, but I'd like that too."

"Be very careful what you say to me," he whispered close to her ear. The light touch of his lips sent delicious tremors of excitement down her spine. "From now on I intend to take you at your word. I intend to take you in every way you'll allow. I want you in every way—in my arms, in my bed, in my home, in my life."

Her heart was doing acrobatics. Her legs were so rubbery that she sagged against him, but he supported her weight easily, even welcomed it, as his mouth moved over hers, teasing its tremulous outline, sampling its sweetness without settling.

Her hands crept toward his shoulders until at last her arms were entwined around his neck. Her fingers were tangled in the thick, springy hair at his temples as she melted into his embrace, allowing her body to conform to the hard contours of his, encouraging him to deepen his kiss.

When Matt pulled away from her and raised his head fractionally, Paige's eyes remained half-closed, focused on his lips as they curved into a satisfied smile that seemed to proclaim victory.

"Irish, say you love me," he instructed.

His voice lingered over her name as tangibly as a caress. Lost in the sight and sound and touch of him, she was ready to pay any forfeit he demanded if only he would kiss her properly.

"You love me," she echoed languidly, and his grin broadened, demonstrating his appreciation of her enraptured confusion.

"And you love me," he declared.

"Yes," she agreed faintly, and was rewarded when his lips fastened greedily on hers.

There was no tenderness in their kiss. There was only an overwhelming need to be close and closer still as they strained together, inflicting sweet punishment on one another with their mouths. He held her so fiercely that she became painfully aware of each of his fingertips digging into the sensitive skin of her back. It was as if he sought to bond her to him permanently through the pressure his hands exerted upon her body.

They were oblivious to time and place until some of the volleyball players happened upon them. Their shrill whistles and the encouragement they shouted brought Matt and Paige back to reality, but it was only a partial reality on Paige's part.

Although darkness was falling rapidly by then and ghostly tentacles of fog were clutching at the shoreline, she could have sworn that the sun was still shining brightly and the heavens were painted with rainbows.

They began walking back the way they'd come. They kept an arm about each other's waists, but their behavior was quite circumspect until they neared the house. Then good behavior was supplanted by desire, and they ran the last hundred yards.

They were laughing breathlessly when Matt closed the front door behind them. For a moment they stood just inside the foyer, staring at each other in wonderment, and suddenly neither of them was laughing.

"Come here," Matt said huskily.

She went into his arms joyfully, and he gathered her close and buried his face in her hair.

"I'd like to make amends for neglecting you the last few days," he whispered roughly, "but I'm not sure how to go about it."

"I have every confidence you'll think of something."

She smiled at Matt trustingly when he raised his head to look down at her. Her eyes were lambent with desire as she cradled his head with her hands and pulled his mouth down to hers. The long, deeply searching kiss they shared left her hungry for more of him. She was intensely aware of his rising passion as his lips left hers to sample the warm hollows at the base of her throat.

Matt's hands were trembling as they caressed her breasts, and he moaned low in his throat when his fingers encountered the tightly budded peaks that tented the soft velour of her pullover. He was shaken by a spasm of longing, and he molded her softness more closely to him, kissing the side of her neck and inhaling her sweet, warm fragrance.

She wrapped her arms around him tightly and for a time they simply held one another. The anticipation of what was going to happen between them added a certain spice to their sweet restraint. It was as if their passion fed upon itself and gained strength, and until the undeniable need for greater intimacies spurred them into motion, they were reluctant to end their embrace even for the brief time it would take to walk from the foyer into the bedroom.

When they entered the dimly lighted bedroom,

their desire had escalated so that the necessity for haste was even more compelling, but by then Paige's hands were trembling so badly that Matt had stripped down to his briefs before she'd had time to remove more than her sneakers.

She was just stepping out of her jeans when Matt stopped her, saying, "Let me help with the rest."

Although his face was taut with urgency, his movements were gentle—almost reverent. He lifted the pullover over her head with exquisite care and sucked in his breath sharply when she stood before him, clad only in delectably seductive wisps of turquoise satin and lace.

"Sweet heaven!" His eyes were dark with passion as they roamed over her. "Is that what you had on under your wedding dress?"

She nodded.

"If I'd known that..."

Matt trailed into silence, leaving the rest of his thought unspoken, but his meaning was clear. If he'd known, they would have found their way to bed long before now.

"Oh, lady!" he exclaimed thickly. "I don't think either of us is going to be doing much sleeping tonight."

His arms went around her and she rested her cheek against his shoulder and kissed the new scar she found there.

"That's a souvenir of Afghanistan," he said gruffly.

His hands felt scaldingly hot when they brushed against her as he unhooked her bra. The scrap of satin and lace fell to the floor unheeded as he kissed and caressed the milky white flesh the brassiere had concealed. He stroked the shell-pink areolas with his thumbs and teased them with his tongue until her nipples were saucily erect and her head was reeling with the sensations he was evoking.

She fell into his arms and together they toppled onto the bed. Further ceremony was forgotten as he hurriedly peeled off her bikini panties and his own briefs, and any thought of restraint was cast aside with the last of their clothing.

Their limbs entwined and they lay tangled together, touching and kissing and tasting, tantalizing each other with hands and lips and tongue as their explorations became more and more intimate.

But for a time after Paige was ready for the ultimate intimacy, Matt deliberately held back. He blazed a feverish line of kisses from her throat to her breasts to her navel, while his hands became increasingly urgent. The liberties he took grew more ardent, more insistent, and when he buried his face against the smooth plain of her belly, her need had become a throbbing ache within her. She was enthralled by him, wild with wanting him, and she pleaded with him to take her.

He moved over her, his body hot and hard and possessive. "Have you any idea," he murmured, "how many times I've dreamed of this moment—dreamed you were with me like this, asking me to make love to you?"

His voice was throaty, an exultant growl, and he penetrated her with an almost primitive urgency, boldly invading the narrow, secret valley, but when they were one, his eager movements became slower, more measured. He brought her to the pinnacle of rapture again and again, while he himself drew back, savoring the wonder and beauty of their lovemaking, wishing it might last forever.

The pleasure he gave her, her own unrestrained response, fueled the flames of his excitement, but still, with hard-won control, he delayed his own release.

It was as if he were demanding to know all of her secrets, and she revealed them willingly, withholding nothing. And only when the last secret had been uncovered, only when Matt had thoroughly explored and celebrated each exciting mystery, did they plunge over the brink and into the long, delicious spiral that transported both of them to the blissful heights of ecstasy.

Chapter Fifteen

As it turned out, Matt was right in his prediction. Neither of them did much sleeping that night. They dozed intermittently and were awakened by their ravenous need for one another. Again and again Matt made love to her, submerging himself with undiminished ardor in the sweet, soft solace of her body.

Paige had never felt so cherished.

It was five o'clock Saturday morning when another kind of hunger overtook them and they remembered they hadn't had dinner the night before. Paige offered to prepare breakfast, but Matt insisted they go out.

When she would have argued, he kissed her into submission. "I'd rather you saved your energies for other things," he admitted candidly. "Besides, I've got a yen for some four-alarm chili."

"What you've got is a cast-iron stomach!" Paige happily retorted.

They threw on some clothes and ventured out into the early morning fog. Matt took her to an all-night café that was only a few minutes drive from his house. Except for some truck drivers and one or two other hardy souls, there were few people about at that hour of the morning, so they very nearly had the place to themselves.

They sat close together on the same side of the booth, and although the café was brightly lighted, Paige saw things through a romantic haze, as if the batting of fog that rubbed against the windowpanes had filtered into the restaurant.

Both of them had ordered mammoth breakfasts, but when desire reasserted itself, by unspoken mutual consent, they left their food half-finished in order to hurry back to the house and to bed.

They spent the rest of Saturday and most of Sunday in the same glorious way. Loving and sleeping and waking to make love again, they shared everything.

They ate at odd hours when the mood struck them. They went for walks on the beach and tarried to watch the volleyball games and the fishermen, the surfers, the joggers, and the body-builders.

Sometimes, in the midst of one of these diversions, Matt would catch her eye and smile, and she could tell that he was thinking about the things they'd do to each other when they were alone again. And she would smile back at him, knowing that before long one of them would suggest they return to the house.

On Saturday afternoon they built a driftwood fire on the beach to roast hot dogs and marshmallows, and later that night, they built another one in the living room fireplace to dispel the dampness of the fog. Then, with sweet words and honeyed kisses and teas-

ing caresses, they struck more volatile sparks in one
another and made love to the accompaniment of one
of Matt's recordings of balalaika music.

They talked together and laughed together. They
discussed their work at some length, and Matt told
her quite a lot about some of the countries he'd seen
in his travels, but they were careful not to permit any
mention of the past to creep into their conversations.
It was as if they had reached a tacit understanding that
the very topics which were of paramount importance
to them had been ruled off-limits.

At times they were surrounded by people, yet they
managed to keep the outside world from intruding until Sunday afternoon. The sun had burned away the
last hint of fog by then and the ocean was a sparkling
indigo blue that reflected the brilliance of the sky.

They had agreed to have a proper meal, and Matt
had broiled some steaks over the charcoal grill on the
deck, while Paige took charge of preparing garlic
bread and putting a salad together.

When she brought her contributions to their picnic
to the built-in table on the deck, Matt inquired half-
seriously, "Are you sure you're ready for this?"

"Looks wonderful," she replied, but she was looking at him and not at the filet mignon he was serving
her.

Correctly interpreting her answer as a compliment
to him, Matt laughingly explained, "I meant are you
ready for my cooking!"

"Oh." Her gaze shifted to the steaks only for an
instant before returning to him. "Well, they look
wonderful too."

Matt had taken special care to prepare her steak exactly as she liked it, and she ate every bite of food on her plate, but it might as well have been sawdust because Matt filled her senses to the exclusion of everything else.

The other night, at Cynthia's party, Paige had recognized that since her aunt's death, she'd been marking time, searching for some justification for seeing Matt again, and now for a few fleeting moments it seemed to Paige that he was everything to her.

He was her teacher, her most treasured companion, her closest confidant. He was her friend, her husband, her lover, her very life.

She felt deliriously happy just being with him—so happy it was frightening—and she was shocked to realize how terribly important Matt was to her. But when the food was gone and they were clearing away the dishes, she regained enough equanimity to promise, "Dinner will be my treat. I can work miracles if you have some cheese—"

"I think I can swing that."

Standing in the kitchen doorway to prevent her leaving the room, Matt trapped her in his arms and dropped a kiss on the tip of her nose. Her hands were flattened against his chest as if to fend off his advances, but she only laughed up at him and inquired, "And some wine?"

"Um-hmmm." Now his lips were moving across her cheek, and she looped her arms around his neck. Her body felt languid, liquid with desire.

"And some stale bread?" she went on.

"I've got lots of that." His lips feathered along the

side of her neck. "That's one thing bachelors usually have plenty of."

"Spinsters, too," she breathed. Relishing this lovely new game of enticement he was playing, she pressed closer to him. "Do you think there's something significant about that?"

"You bet," he growled, underscoring his answer with a biting little kiss on her earlobe. "It means that, since we're married now, never again will we have to worry about how to get rid of all that stale bread."

"Matt!"

She had intended her intonation of his name to sound like a rebuke, but her voice dwindled to a sigh when he began delving into the tiny recesses of her ear with the tip of his tongue. He felt her shudder with pleasure and folded her even closer to him.

"I can work miracles too," he said delightedly. "All it takes is a few minutes alone with you, and I don't even need cheese or wine or bread."

"So you can." She nestled into his arms and rubbed her cheek against his shoulder before she added impudently, "But I'll bet you can't make a fondue without them."

"Irish, sweetheart, who cares?"

He fitted her hips to his and moved his body against hers in a sensuous way that left her in no doubt as to his intentions, and faced with such compelling logic she willingly surrendered to his superior arguments.

"Who indeed?" she challenged provocatively as she rose onto her tiptoes to kiss him on the mouth.

Laughing raggedly, Matt swung her off her feet and carried her toward the bedroom.

"You never did tell me who that guy was," said Matt sometime later.

They were lounging on the deck in the warm late afternoon sun and Paige was trying to sketch him. She glanced inquiringly at him around the edge of her sketch pad.

"What guy?" she asked.

"The one you spent so much time with the other night at Cynthia's."

Her hand faltered when Matt mentioned Cynthia and the proud flare of the nostril she was drawing came out all squiggly.

"That was Derek—Derek—" Her memory failed her, and after a momentary pause, she said, "I'm sorry, but I can't seem to come up with his last name. Is it important?"

"Not if you don't remember his full name," Matt drawled sardonically.

Paige glanced at him again, this time suspiciously. She was disappointed when she saw that he appeared to be amused rather than jealous. She reached for her eraser and sighed, which prompted Matt to flip his sunglasses up to his forehead and look at her intently.

"What was the sigh for?" he asked.

"I—I don't know. It's just that—well, you've known an awful lot of women—"

"Not as many as you seem to think," he interposed dryly.

"Even so—"

"Look, Irish," he broke in more brusquely now, "I haven't asked you what you've been up to all these years."

"N-no, I know you haven't."

She was grateful for that because the years without him had been so uneventful that it was embarrassing. Her face grew hot with color at the recollection of how chaste she had been, and she ducked behind the sketch pad and busied herself with her drawing to hide the fact that she was blushing.

"Irish," Matt remarked incredulously, "surely you can't be fretting because you're not the first woman I've known."

"Not as long as I'm the last!" she declared vehemently.

Despite the gentle nature of his chiding, her fingers had clenched around her pencil so fiercely that she'd broken the point, making a jagged tear in the paper in the process. As she removed the page from the tablet, Matt held his hand out to her.

"Let's see it," he requested.

She looked at him blankly for a few seconds before she realized he was referring to her sketch. She handed it to him silently and watched him break into a smile as he studied it.

"Not bad." Matt grinned more widely as he held the drawing at arms length and closed one eye. Looking at her effort from this new perspective, he said lightly, "It's even better with one eye closed."

"Try it with both eyes closed," Paige suggested.

"Or how about like this?" he inquired, crossing his eyes at her.

She was reduced to helpless laughter by his mugging as he turned the drawing sideways and upside down, assessing it from every conceivable angle, and for a time the tension that had ruffled the surface calm of their idyll was smoothed over.

It was not until later that Paige began to wonder why Matt had not responded to the question that was implicit in her comment about being the last woman in his life.

The knowledge that Matt had undoubtedly slept with some of the women he'd dated when she'd first known him at Stanford had never troubled her. And she wasn't bothered by whatever nameless, faceless women he might have had affairs with since then. But in the case of Cynthia Waring the situation was different.

If Derek's analysis could be relied upon, Cynthia hadn't succeeded in adding Matt's name to her list of conquests. Paige wasn't even sure that Cynthia and Matt had been lovers. But Cynthia was neither nameless nor faceless. She was here and she was now and, above all else, she was threatening.

Only twenty-four hours later, Paige would discover just how threatening.

It was the next afternoon, when Paige returned to the house from a walk on the beach, that she found Cynthia there, waiting for her.

Paige entered the house the same way she'd left it, through the sliding glass doors leading from the living room to the deck. She was latching the screen when she heard a noise—as if someone had closed one of the drawers of the linen cupboard in the master bathroom.

As soon as she heard the sound, she froze. Had

Matt managed to get away from the office and come home early? she wondered. But no, it couldn't be Matt in the bathroom. There had been something stealthy about the way the drawer was closed.

She had remained immobile for a full minute before she heard the faint but unmistakable sound of footsteps coming from the bedroom. They were also furtive and definitely not like Matt's firm stride.

Now that she was certain Matt was not responsible for the noises, her first thought was that she shouldn't have left the house unlocked and unattended. Granted the front door had been locked, but she'd left the sliding door open, and that was tantamount to hanging out a sign, asking for a break-in.

Her gaze skidded about the room, but nothing seemed to have been disturbed. Even the statue of *Kuan Yin* was in its usual niche near the fireplace. But would an average, run-of-the-mill burglar recognize its value?

Paige's next thought was that she should just open the screen door and leave again, as quickly and quietly as possible, before the thief or prowler or whoever was in the bedroom had the opportunity to learn of her presence.

Then she was gripped by a sense of violation. Anger took hold at the idea that some total stranger might have been pawing through her personal belongings, and she told herself, *This is my home, and I'm not going to let some creep run me out of it!*

She was filled with determination that, if anyone was going to run away, it was not going to be she. She also felt the first twinges of fear, but even if she might have changed her mind, she had no chance for second thoughts. While she'd been trying to decide what action she should take, the trespasser had left the bedroom and was coming up the stairs toward the living room.

"Wh-who's there?" she called out as firmly as she could, before her fear could blossom any further.

There was a trill of musical laughter, and in the next moment Cynthia appeared in the doorway to the hall on the far side of the living room. Her eyes darted over Paige in swift, calculating appraisal, taking in the most minute details of Paige's rolled-up jeans and bare, sandy feet.

As usual, Cynthia was impeccably turned out. She was wearing a chic, parchment-colored dress that quite obviously had not been purchased off the rack, and although it was a warm day, a fur coat was draped with casual elegance over her shoulders.

The sable-dark pelts of the fur contrasted dramatically with Cynthia's ash-blond hair. Furthermore, she toned so perfectly with the decor of the room that she looked as if it was she who belonged in Matt's house and Paige who was the interloper.

To counteract this impression, Paige moved away from the sliding doors and seated herself on the sofa. Not to be outdone, Cynthia followed suit, striking a feline pose by perching on the arm of one of the easy chairs as she said, "I'm sorry I frightened you. I had no idea you were here."

Ignoring Cynthia's apology, Paige announced woodenly, "Matt's not here. He had to go in to the office."

"I'm well aware of that, darling. I saw him less than half an hour ago."

"How did you get in, Cynthia?"

"With my key, naturally." Smiling triumphantly at the look of consternation on Paige's face, she added, "I assure you, I did knock, but when there was no answer, I simply let myself in. It seemed the only sensible thing to do since I needed to collect a few, er, things I'd left here."

An icy rage seized Paige. Inwardly she was trembling, seething with anger because Matt hadn't yet offered to provide her with a key to the house, but her voice revealed none of her emotional turmoil as she asked steadily, "And have you collected them?"

"Why, yes."

Momentary surprise flickered in Cynthia's eyes at Paige's composed response. Her ambiguous use of the word *things* to describe the articles she had supposedly come to get had been an open invitation to inquiry, yet Paige had not given her the satisfaction of asking her to itemize them.

"Yes," Cynthia repeated. With a blithe wave of her hand, she indicated the carryall she'd left beside the entry to the hall. "As a matter of fact, I was just finishing up when I heard you come in."

"In that case, I'd suggest you take them and be on your way." Paige nodded coolly at her uninvited visitor, got to her feet and started walking across the living room toward the hall. "Oh, and you'd better leave your key behind," she added firmly. "It will save me the trouble of having the locks changed."

"Why you little— How dare you!" Cynthia sputtered. "You can't dismiss me so easily!"

Without slowing her step, Paige retorted smoothly, "Oh, can't I? Just watch me!"

Cynthia gasped with shock. "It's me Matt really loves," she cried stridently. "I mean more to him than you ever will!"

Succumbing to temptation, Paige stopped beneath the archway to the hall. She turned to look at Cynthia as she remarked, "Everyone's entitled to one mistake, and I guess you're Matt's, but I'm willing to overlook it."

"Damn you to hell, Paige Cavanaugh! You mean nothing to Matt. Do you hear? *Nothing*!" When Paige left the doorway, Cynthia shrieked, "If you walk out on me now, you'll live to regret it! I promise you will—"

Pursued by Cynthia's dire predictions, Paige continued along the hallway. She knew that Cynthia had come to the doorway and was watching her. The hair at the back of her neck prickled and the area between her shoulder blades seemed to crawl with the stabbing malevolence of the other woman's gaze, but she forced herself to maintain an unhurried, almost sauntering pace until she had reached the sanctuary of the bedroom.

Once inside, she quickly closed the door behind her and collapsed against it. She stood there while Cynthia's shrill tirade trailed into an ominous silence, inhaling deeply in an effort to stem the nausea that was churning at the back of her throat.

The musky-spicy scent of Cynthia's perfume lingered in the bedroom, overpowering the subtler fragrance of the daffodils Paige had arranged on the nightstand, and she hurried to the windows and opened them wide.

Finally she heard Cynthia slam out of the house, and a few moments later, the low rumble of a car engine. Cynthia gunned the motor furiously as she drove away, but even when nothing more than the soothing sigh of the surf and the occasional cry of a sea-bird disturbed the silence in the bedroom, Paige didn't stir. She leaned against the windowsill, too shaken to move.

She was not so gullible that she accepted all of Cynthia's claims at face value, yet she was tormented by the feeling that somewhere, camouflaged by the barrage of lies Cynthia had spouted, there must be a grain of truth.

The key, for instance. She was positive Cynthia hadn't lied about that. But which of Cynthia's other pronouncements should she believe?

That Cynthia had just come from Matt?

Yes, Paige reluctantly decided. That had had a ring of honesty about it.

That she had come to collect something of a personal nature which she'd left here at some time or other?

Perhaps this was the truth, although Paige had seen nothing that was even remotely recognizable as Cynthia's in the time she'd spent here.

That Matt loved Cynthia?

No! She *refused* to believe that.

She did, however, believe that Cynthia was in love with Matt. She must love him deeply to have taken such a desperate course of action.

Suddenly, Paige regretted that she'd let her pride stop her from finding out exactly what Cynthia had come to collect. They might have offered some clue to Matt's feelings for the other woman. Was Cynthia the woman he loved, or was she a woman he'd scorned?

And what about his feelings for me? she wondered.

Early that morning, when Judy Garcia had called to inform them that something had come up that required Matt's immediate attention, he'd been apologetic about having to go to the office today. He'd seemed sincere when he'd said he hated to leave her.

And throughout their weekend together he'd been unfailingly sweet to her. He'd been the most delightfully amusing companion imaginable, and the most demanding, exciting, considerate lover. Their lovemaking had been beautiful. So tender. So right.

Matt had said only that he wanted her, never that he loved her, but surely he must feel some affection for her. He couldn't have faked the passion he'd shown her.

Or could he?

Chapter Sixteen

As impossible as it seemed, only that morning Paige had decided that the third-day anniversary of their wedding called for a very special dinner that night. She had gone shopping, and without a thought for the extravagance of the gesture, she'd bought lobster and dozens of candles and a bottle of vintage Chardonnay. On the way back to the house, she'd stopped at one of the curbside vendors and purchased armloads of spring flowers.

Before Cynthia's arrival she had set the table in the dining room with some heirloom china and crystal she'd found hidden away in a kitchen cupboard. She had lovingly arranged the flowers, creating a centerpiece for the table with the lilacs and hyacinths. She had separated the tulips and daffodils into smaller bouquets and scattered them throughout the rest of the house.

The candles were ready to light, the lobster was ready to slide under the broiler, and the wine was perfectly chilled, but her heart was no longer in the festivities she'd planned.

For all of her agonizing over Cynthia's motives in coming to the house, she was sure of only one thing. Cynthia wanted Matt. Therefore it followed that Cynthia's purpose in paying her a visit had been to make trouble between Matt and her.

The only bright spot in having arrived at these conclusions was the knowledge that the only way the other woman's scheme could succeed was if she, Paige, were to lose faith in Matt.

But, she decided firmly, she'd be damned if she'd let Cynthia succeed.

By the time Matt came home, Paige had regained control of her truant thoughts, and of her emotions. She was just stepping out of the shower when she heard his car in the driveway, and she slipped into her dressing gown and hurriedly tied it about her waist.

Matt let himself into the house and called for her.

"Irish," he called, "where's my wife?"

"In here, Matt," she cried.

Her hand shook as she pulled her hairbrush through the tangles in her hair, but the barely suppressed excitement she had heard in Matt's voice added to her resolve. Without further hesitation, she left the bathroom to meet him.

He was standing in the bedroom doorway. His arms were outstretched, as if he were eager to hold her, and she ran into them. Going onto her tiptoes, she raised her lips to his. She kissed him fervently, responding so hungrily to the warm pressure of his mouth that her skin was scoured by the stubble of his beard.

"Good lord," he murmured against her lips. "To what do I owe this seductive greeting?"

Paige touched the tip of her tongue to his before she answered. "Matthew Jonas," she chided him softly. "At a time like this, how can you be so grammatical?"

Matt chuckled. "Sorry, sweetness, it's habit. Remaining grammatical under stress is one of the occupational hazards of being a journalist."

She trailed a teasing line of kisses along the angle of his jaw. "You consider this stress?"

"Ummm." He stopped her exploring lips with a quick, ardent kiss. "The nicest kind of stress."

"Does that mean you don't like it?"

"I love it," he growled, "but why—"

"I missed you today, that's all."

"In that case," Matt said thickly as he untied the belt of her robe, "I'll have to leave home more often."

His mouth was almost savage with urgency as it claimed hers again, but his hands moved over her slowly, roving upward from her waist until they arrived at the delicate undercurve of her breasts.

Her breasts were still tender from his lovemaking, and already they were heavy with desire. Her nipples were rosy and tingling, and even before Matt touched them they had become swollen and erect with the mere anticipation of his caresses.

She ached for his touch and, as if he sensed her innermost needs, Matt began teasing the nipples with his fingertips, tracing slow circles around them. He was infinitely gentle and she arched into the tantalizing eroticism of his touch, sighing softly with the pleasure he gave her. Her mouth opened wider to receive the sweet glide of his tongue, and he held her even more closely to him, molding her hips to his.

She recognized that he was fully aroused and in the next moment he had lifted her off her feet and tumbled her onto the bed. He followed after her, pinning her to the mattress with the delicious weight of his body, and she embraced him blissfully.

She was returning Matt's kisses and caressing him wildly, quickening to his tempo, when the now familiar scent of Cynthia's perfume penetrated the all-consuming heat of her desire. And when she realized that the scent was coming from Matt's shirt, when she became aware that the fragrance Cynthia used clung to Matt's skin, her doubts returned in a dizzying rush.

Despite the cloying reminder of Cynthia's visit, for a time her woman's body continued to respond to Matt's lovemaking. She still wanted him. She wanted him so badly that her craving had become a tempest raging deep inside her. But her mind was strangely divorced from her body. It was entirely clear and was functioning efficiently.

She knew with painful clarity that Cynthia had won. She knew that she had passed through the fires of passion and arrived at the final, irrevocable reality. She had been tempered by the fire, and she was perfectly, icily detached. She felt as if she were only a bystander witnessing the love scene in the bedroom. She became so uninvolved, it was as though Matt wasn't actually making love to her.

How could he? The question screamed through her mind. How *dared* he come straight from Cynthia's arms to hers?

She began struggling to escape his hold on her, but her struggles were weak and ineffective against his strength. Only minutes before, the virile thrust of his body against hers had been exciting, an aphrodisiac. Now his rock-hard chest was a suffocating weight that crushed the softness of her breasts and denied her breath. The sinewy muscles in his arms were as un-yielding as iron bands.

But his hands were gentle and his lips continued wooing her. Against her will, her body responded to the sweet tug of his mouth upon her breast.

She sensed that Matt thought her pathetic struggles were some sort of game she was playing. She sensed that they served only to further inflame him, and as a last resort, she schooled herself to lie limp and acqui-escent beneath him.

Within moments it became apparent that this strat-egy was going to have the desired effect. She knew she should have been relieved, but when she felt Matt's reaction to her inertia, when he tensed and rolled away from her and dragged himself off the bed, she felt like weeping.

He stalked to the door before he turned to look at her. His eyes were coldly speculative as they traveled over her, making her acutely conscious of her naked-ness. He left the room without speaking, but Paige had seen the taut set of his jaw. She'd felt the destruc-tive force of his anger. She knew he'd had to leave the room or smash something. She knew that when his anger had leveled off, when it had reached manageable proportions, he would be back.

When Paige heard him walking along the hall in the direction of the living room, she got shakily to her feet and wrapped herself in her dressing gown. She tied the belt snugly about her waist, then knotted it again, as if the robe afforded her some kind of shield against Matt's anger.

She only wished it were as easy to wrap herself once again in the ephemeral security of her illusions about their marriage.

At this thought, her knees buckled. She slumped onto the side of the bed and buried her face in her hands. She had no conception of how much time had passed before Matt reappeared in the doorway of the bedroom. As she raised her head to return his gaze, she felt unreal, as if she had been trapped in a waking nightmare.

Matt was carrying a half-empty glass of whiskey in one lean hand. The glass dangled loosely from the tips of his fingers, as if he'd forgotten he had it. He held his arms stiffly at his sides as he stood in the doorway, confronting Paige as warily as if they were not husband and wife, but adversaries; as if the intimacies they'd shared had never been.

When he had maneuvered Paige into accepting his proposal, he'd thought he would be content if he could have her on his terms. By their wedding day, he'd known that he wanted her on any terms. Their weekend honeymoon had taught him that he would never be satisfied just to possess her physically.

No matter what she'd done, no matter how she'd

lied, he loved her, and above all else, he wanted her to care for him as much as he cared for her.

The skeptic in Matt told him he was a besotted fool. His masculine pride counseled him not to let Paige get away with turning the tables on him. But the time for warnings was past. It was too late for retaliation because he'd already lost Paige.

This realization filled him with uncertainty, and in his dealings with women, Matt was not accustomed to anything less than total self-assurance.

Perhaps this was why he didn't feel Paige's uncertainty. He felt only the chilly air of formality with which she had cloaked her own doubts. He didn't see that she had lost the warmly radiant look of a woman who knows she is loved. He saw only her reserve. And something else shimmered in the cool sea-green depths of her eyes. Was it fear?

He downed the last of the whiskey in a single long swallow and saluted her with the empty glass.

"There's no need to be afraid, Irish," he said mockingly. "I'm not sure what you were trying to prove by giving me the big come-on, then turning it into a runaround, but you've been granted a last minute reprieve. If there's one thing I can't take, it's being tolerated."

His voice had roughened with the violence of his emotions, and he paused, striving to regain control of himself.

"Let me assure you," he drawled, "making love to an unwilling woman is not my idea of a fun way to spend the evening. The only reason I came back is to tell you I heard from Mitzi Vaughn today."

Paige stared at Matt mutely, wondering why she should have such a strange sinking sensation in the pit of her stomach. Shouldn't she be pleased that her search might be nearing its end?

Then she saw the fiery glint in Matt's eyes and she attributed her anxiety to his forbidding expression. Her pride would not let her admit, even to herself, that she was frightened because he'd spoken to Mitzi. Inwardly, she was quaking with fear that if they found Stella, if Stella offered substantiation that their baby had been stillborn, Matt would have no reason at all to continue on in their marriage.

"Mitzi stopped by the office about an hour ago," Matt went on coolly. "She pulled some strings and managed to come up with Stella's address."

"Wh-where is Stella?"

"Evidently she's given up the kennel business. She's living on a houseboat in Sausalito."

Unable to believe she'd heard Matt correctly, Paige shook her head. "Do you mean—"

"That's right, Irish." His tone was ironic. "All these weeks you've been frantically trying to find Stella, and the whole time she's been living less than ten miles from Mill Valley. You probably could have looked her up in your phone book."

"No..." Paige murmured shakily. "If only I'd known. It never even occurred to me that she might be that near by."

"Obviously," Matt retorted grimly.

His eyes, his tone of voice, the way he had positioned himself so inflexibly in the doorway, everything about him seemed to be accusing her of something. Did he think she had known Stella's whereabouts all along?

"What—" She was dry-mouthed and her voice was raspy. She paused to lick her lips before she finished asking, "What do you think we should do now?"

Matt shrugged. "That depends on you. Mitzi gave me Stella's phone number. We could try calling her. Or if you prefer, we could take a run up to Sausalito and see her."

He was watching her with such hawklike intensity that she felt increasingly uneasy. Attempting to appear nonchalant, she got to her feet, crossed to the dresser, and began combing her hair.

"I think it would be best to see her." That's better, she thought, thankful that she sounded a bit more confident now. "I mean, it is a delicate matter—"

"That's putting it mildly."

Startled by the skepticism she heard in Matt's voice, she glanced at him in the mirror. He had moved away from the door and was striding lithely across the room, but when she spun around to face him, she was taken aback to find him so close to her.

"I can make the trip by myself," she hastily volunteered. "You needn't come along."

"Oh, I needn't, huh?"

With deceptive gentleness, Matt cupped her chin with his hand and tipped her head back, forcing her to submit to his scrutiny. He looked at her derisively as she stood, white-faced and trembling, trapped between his hard-muscled body and the bureau at her back.

"Y-you sound as if you don't trust me."

Matt's fingers tightened until his hold on her chin was very nearly punishing. "That's very perceptive. I don't."

"What is it you think I might do?" she asked thickly. It was difficult to get the words out when he was gripping her jaw so prohibitively.

"Give it up," he advised her silkily. "You're not deceiving me with your act of big-eyed innocence. Oh, I'll admit that for a while there you had me fooled, but you shouldn't have pulled the stunt you did when I got home tonight."

Matt shook his head reproachfully. "Frankly, my dear, I expected you to be more resourceful. I'd have thought it would be beneath your dignity to tip your hand that way, but you underestimated my intelligence. Did you think I'd be so blinded by lust for you that I wouldn't see what you were up to? Did you do it because I didn't take you to bed the moment I saw you again? Couldn't you wait to get even with me for finding you resistible? Was that it? Or was it that you couldn't pass up the opportunity to take an extra pound of flesh out of my hide?"

Paige opened her mouth to respond to Matt's charges, but his sardonic smile silenced her.

"Cat got your tongue?" he taunted. "Ah, well, it doesn't matter. You might have the face of an angel, but in my opinion, underneath it all you're the most vindictive, conniving female I've ever had the misfortune to meet. I know damned well there's nothing you'd like better than for me to fall in with your offer to see Stella alone. That way, if our daughter is alive, you could pick her up and ride off into the sunset without the inconvenience of a husband to cramp your style. You'd just disappear."

"I wouldn't, Matt! I swear I wouldn't."

"Come off it, Irish."

The uncompromising jut of his chin, the cynical lift of his eyebrows made it plain that he hadn't believed her belated protest. She tried to pull away from him, but he coiled his free arm about her waist and hauled her closer to him, binding her softness to the strong length of his thighs.

"It might interest you to know that when you showed me the clipping and told me about the baby, my first impulse was to wring your pretty little neck for you." As if to illustrate how tempting this idea had been, Matt's fingers slid from her chin and fastened lightly around her throat.

"But after I'd had time to cool off and think it over," he went on dispassionately, "it seemed to me that would be too merciful, considering the enormity of what you'd done to me. That was when I decided it would be a lot more satisfying to indulge you by giving you exactly what you were angling for—although not quite in the openhanded way you had in mind— and watch you try to squirm out of keeping your end of the bargain."

Paige felt as if she were in shock. She wanted to hide her eyes and cover her ears, to shut out Matt's indictment of her. But more than anything else, as if Matt's charges were a self-fulfilling prophecy, she wanted to strike back at him, to hurt him as much as he'd hurt her.

"Don't expect any gratitude for your show of leniency," she lashed out. Her voice sounded brittle and far away. "You were right, you know. In some ways, being married to you is worse than a death sentence."

"Touché!" Matt laughed bitterly and a little hoarsely at her rejoinder, but his expression was enigmatic as he said, "I suppose we might as well play out this farce so we can put the whole ludicrous episode behind us. We'll leave for Sausalito first thing in the morning."

Chapter Seventeen

Paige had never felt as completely alone as she did during the drive along the coast to Sausalito. Although Matt was in the driver's seat, only a foot away from her at most, either he was lost in thought or staring intently at the highway ahead.

They set out even before sunrise. Neither of them had slept very much the night before, and they never had gotten around to eating the lobster or drinking the wine.

After their final antagonistic exchange, Matt had left the house. Paige didn't know where he'd gone, but wherever it was, it had been diverting enough that he hadn't returned till after midnight. She desperately wanted to know whether he'd spent the evening with Cynthia, but he didn't say where he'd been, and after his comment about "putting the whole ludicrous episode behind them," she didn't feel she had any right to keep tabs on him.

If anything, the constraint between them was even stronger and more oppressive this morning. Paige was reduced to a tongue-tied stammer if Matt so much as glanced in her direction. She barely managed to reply if he spoke to her, which was no more often than was absolutely necessary, and she didn't attempt to initiate any conversation.

Matt's car was an almost new Audi-5000. He drove with a deft economy of motion at a fast, even speed, so they traveled the three hundred miles in good time, yet the awkward silence between them made the journey seem endless.

Because they had stopped for a late breakfast in Salinas, they didn't reach the San Francisco Peninsula until shortly after noon.

"Aren't you going to stop in and see your mother?" she asked when Matt drove by the last of the Palo Alto exits without even slowing down.

Without taking his eyes off the road, he replied, "Maybe on the way back. They aren't expecting us."

She glanced at him curiously, wondering if he was still at odds with Professor Jonas. It seemed a shame he wasn't going to see his mother, especially since they were only a few miles from his parents' home.

"It must be hard for your mother—" she began tentatively.

"It's harder for her if I come by without an invitation," Matt interrupted.

"Is your stepfather still jealous of you?"

"It's not just me. Doc has become much more possessive of my mother since she had her stroke. He prefers to have her all to himself. He tends to sulk if she has any unannounced visitors."

"I'm sorry to hear that," Paige said huskily. "Your mother was always so interested in people, so gregarious. She seemed to love entertaining and having crowds of friends around her. How does she manage to . . . cope?"

"She understands Doc." Matt shrugged. "I guess she loves him enough to make the sacrifice. At any rate, she defers to him in that she discourages uninvited guests."

"I'm sorry," Paige repeated inadequately. Not only was she expressing her sympathy for his mother's problem, she was also apologizing to Matt for her lack of insight into his relationship with his parents.

What was it he'd said last night? She couldn't remember exactly, but she was positive it had been something about not being able to take being tolerated. At the time she'd been wallowing in her own misery and it hadn't really sunk in, but now it occurred to her that in at least one respect, her upbringing and Matt's had had their similarities.

Both of them had knocked themselves out trying to win the approval of one of the most influential adults in their young lives, and through no fault of their own—because of an accident of birth—neither of them had been terribly successful at it.

All at once she wished she could turn the clock back to last night and replay the evening with Matt from the moment of his homecoming.

If only that were possible, she would do things so very differently. She would tell Matt that Cynthia had called on her and ask him for an explanation. Or maybe she'd make a joke out of Cynthia's visit and she and Matt would laugh about how foolish and unnecessary her jealousy was.

And when Matt wanted to make love to her—

But that's not possible, Paige admonished herself sternly. She couldn't go back, and she wasn't sure she wanted to go forward.

After stealing another glance at Matt's craggy profile, she concentrated fixedly on the familiar landmarks rushing by. With each mile they covered, the traffic on the Bayshore Freeway was becoming heavier, and soon the urban sprawl of the Peninsula gave way to high rises and office complexes.

They passed turnoffs for Tanforan and the airport, for the Cow Palace and Candlestick Park. They arrived at one of the layered cloverleaf interchanges that San Franciscans detest so much, and the skyline of the city shimmered before them beneath the crisp blue backdrop of the springtime sky.

Matt stayed on Highway 101, taking Van Ness to Lombard. They were nearing the Golden Gate Bridge and neither of them had spoken again. The silence in the car was almost palpable. It seemed to have developed a character all its own, to hum along on its own high-pitched frequency.

Paige kept her eyes trained on the townhouses that lined the street, looking for some evidence of occupancy. It was something she customarily did when she happened to come through the Pacific Heights district.

The resplendent, multistoried mansions were tastefully and expensively furnished. Without exception, the draperies on the expansive windows facing the Yacht Club and the bay had been left open, allowing passersby a glimpse of the opulence within.

And, also without exception, there was not a sign of human habitation. The rooms she saw were unnaturally neat and totally deserted.

They're empty, she thought. *As empty as my life is going to be without Matt.*

The monotonous thrum of the tires against the pavement as they sped across the Golden Gate Bridge seconded this assessment.

Empty, they seemed to taunt her. *Empty, empty, empty.*

There were two basic types of houseboats anchored along the bayshore in Sausalito: the luxurious, palatial kind, and those that resembled floating shacks. Stella Ackerman lived in one of the latter.

They called at half a dozen or more, each more dilapidated than the one before. At last they found someone who grudgingly directed them to Stella's.

For some reason, Stella had christened her houseboat the *Shangri-La*. It was built of tarpaper and corrugated metal, and judging by the exterior, it was the worst of the lot, but that misnomer was prominently stenciled across one wall of the slant-roofed cabin.

The cabin was little more than a lean-to really, but on the inside, it was surprisingly homey. It was teak-paneled and trimmed with gleaming bright-work that was polished to a fare-thee-well. When Matt complimented her on it, Stella proudly explained that she'd salvaged most of the interior materials from a yacht that had run aground in a fog.

"Not to wish anyone ill," she joked, "but if

another one were to run aground, I might be able to finish the exterior."

Stella herself was remarkably unchanged. Perhaps she was a bit less sprightly and a bit more hard of hearing, but she still wore a man's shirt, twill pants, and knee boots. Her severe iron-gray bob was the same, and her snapping brown eyes still had the same alert and lively sparkle.

The cabin of the houseboat had much the same smell as her house at the kennel, too; a pungent, oddly evocative blend of dog and liniment, woodsmoke and fresh air.

Stella greeted them effusively, led them into her living quarters, and shooed a Saint Bernard out of one of the chairs.

"I like it here well enough," she declared as they seated themselves around the woodburning heater. "Of course it has its disadvantages, but that's true of most anywhere these days. The thing I like best about living here is that I'm such a pain in the ass to the powers that be. They'd like nothing better than to get rid of us squatters but so far they haven't come up with any way short of mayhem of doing it."

Matt grinned appreciatively at her outspokenness, and Stella gave him a conspiratorial wink as she added, "That's the thing I always liked about Paige, here. She's a rebel too, and I admire the way she picks and chooses what to take a stand against. Seems to me, that's a lost art among the younger generation. Most rebels are like me, protesting just on general principles, spinning their wheels and wasting a lot of

energy—and getting knocked in the head by the estab-
lishment for their troubles. They chased me out of my
old place, you know."

"No, I didn't know," Paige exclaimed. "How
could they do something like that?"

"Changed the zoning on me," Stella disclosed
matter-of-factly. "Said the kennel was standing in the
way of progress. Leastways, that was the excuse they
gave. Can you believe it?" she continued irately. "I
lived there close to thirty years, and one fine day, without so much as a by-your-leave, these crummy bastards
from the planning commission waltz in and tell me
they've voted to rewrite the zoning ordinances! And do
you know what they built there, smack-dab in the
middle of nowhere? A drive-in movie theater, that's
what! And they call that progress!"

"How did they force you to leave?" asked Matt.
"Even if they changed the zoning, compliance should
have been waived for as long as you owned the property."

With some embarrassment, Stella replied, "To tell
the truth, the kennel was getting to be too much for
me. I was ready enough to move on."

"What about the cemetery?" Paige inquired anxiously.

"Oh, the family plot is still there," said Stella. "It
takes an Act of Congress—maybe even an act of God—
for a cemetery to be moved, and I insisted that it
shouldn't be touched. But as to the rest, I didn't feel
up to fighting them over it. Guess I'm getting old."

She gave a disgruntled snort that brought the dogs
running to her side at a gallop.

"Settle down, guys, settle down," Stella shouted, patting each of the Saint Bernards in turn. When that had no effect, she roared, "I said settle down, damn it!"

Naturally they didn't obey her—not until she'd bribed them with dog biscuits.

"I do miss the rest of my dogs though," Stella went on forlornly as she returned to her chair. "When I was younger, I used to make fun of all the old ladies who treated their pets as if they were their children, and here I am doing the same thing. But I can only keep a couple of dogs on board, so those two are it."

"They seem to keep you fairly busy though," Matt observed.

"Yeah," Stella chuckled, "that's the truth." She glanced quizzically from Matt to Paige and back to Matt. "I didn't catch your name, young fella."

"This is Matthew Jonas," said Paige.

"So this is Matt." Stella nodded sagely and informed him, "I've heard a lot about you, Matt. It's a real pleasure to meet you after all this time."

Matt's face registered both surprise and perplexity as he replied, "I'm happy to meet you too, Stella."

"I hate to imagine what Paige must have told you about me!" said Stella.

"She's very fond of you, and very grateful," Matt countered gravely. His manner with the elderly woman was quite charming, and Paige noticed with some amusement that Stella was not immune to his appeal. She was fluffing her hair and smoothing her shirt over her ample hips, virtually preening herself.

"I wasn't aware that Paige had told you about me," Matt amended casually, as if he didn't expect Stella to respond to his comment.

But Paige sensed his intensity and quickly inserted, "Neither was I." Without pausing, she rushed into a new topic of conversation. "I wish I'd known you were in Sausalito, Stella. I live in Mill Valley, so we're practically neighbors."

"Didn't your aunt tell you I'd moved here?"

"No, she never mentioned it. But then, we didn't see very much of each other the last few years."

"I haven't heard from Rachel for quite a while myself," said Stella. "How is she, anyway? Still the same old fussbudget?" In an aside to Matt, Stella explained, "Talk about prim! I always thought Rachel Cavanaugh could have posed as the farmer's wife in that painting—you know, the one with the pitchfork. I think it's by Grant Wood."

"*American Gothic*?" Matt provided.

"Yeah, that's the one!" Stella slapped her knee and laughed hilariously until she noticed that she was the only one who saw the humor in the aptness of her comparison. Then she shifted uneasily in her chair. In what was for her a subdued voice, she asked, "Did I say something wrong?"

"I'm sorry to have to tell you this," Matt replied sympathetically, "but Paige's aunt died several months ago."

The normally florid color drained from Stella's face, leaving it a waxen, pasty white. She muttered an oath and fell back into her chair, shaking her head as if she would disavow the news of her friend's death.

"Rachel?" she murmured. "I can't believe it. I simply cannot believe it."

Paige dropped to her knees beside Stella's chair. "Can I get you anything? A glass of water, or some tea?"

"No, dear, not just now."

She patted Paige's hand in much the same way as she had patted the Saint Bernards, and for the first time, she noticed Paige's wedding ring.

"You're married!" she exclaimed, staring with some astonishment at Matt.

"That's right," Matt replied. "We were married on Friday."

"Well, I'll be . . ." Stella's face was suddenly wreathed with smiles. She caught Paige close and hugged her warmly. "Now I don't know whether to mourn or celebrate!"

"I'll settle for one of those hugs," Matt teased.

"You've got it!" Stella shouted, releasing Paige and capturing Matt. "Boy, have you got it!"

Laughing, Matt gave Stella an enthusiastic kiss on the cheek. "I'm glad you approve."

"How could I not approve? Let me tell you—" Stopping abruptly, Stella glanced uncertainly at Paige. "This calls for something a little stronger than tea. Would you mind very much, dear, if I asked you to pour out a tot of my plum brandy for each of us?"

"Of course I wouldn't mind."

"Good, good! There's a locker forward. I think I might have stowed it there." Paige automatically got to her feet and started toward the door leading to the deck. "If it's not there," Stella called after her, "it could be in one of the lockers aft. Just keep looking. You'll find it.''

Only then did Paige begin to suspect that Stella had very neatly gotten her out of the way so that she could talk privately with Matt.

Her suspicions were magnified when she searched the forward locker and found that it was filled with hand tools, firewood, and cans of paint and spar varnish. *Why the old faker!* she thought fondly. She would bet that Stella's plum brandy was nowhere near this part of the houseboat. She'd bet it was safely tucked away inside the cabin.

Ten minutes had gone by before Paige knew without a doubt that she had won her bet. She'd looked in every nook and cranny accessible from the deck without finding a trace of Stella's homemade brandy, and she wondered why she had gone along with the ruse. And why, even now, she felt a strange reluctance to go back inside.

The moment she did go inside, her questions were answered. She saw the way Matt and Stella were sitting with their heads so close together. She saw that they were silent and solemn. She saw the way Stella avoided looking at her.

In a small voice, she said to Matt, ''You asked her about the baby?''

''Yes, Irish.''

''You showed her the clipping?''

Matt nodded. He was pale beneath his tan, and his dark eyes were clouded with anguish. His face was rigidly set, his expression stricken.

He looked, she thought, absolutely desolate—or

was it only that she saw him through a blur of tears as he rose and came toward her? When he took her in his arms, she leaned against him wearily.

"I'm sorry," he said gruffly, "but it was the recipe all along. Stella sent the clipping to your aunt years before the baby was born."

A cleansing wave of sorrow welled up within Paige. At last, she gave herself over to a healing storm of tears.

"I knew it, Matt!" she cried. "I guess I've *always* known. I just couldn't admit it to myself."

Matt hugged her close, absorbing the sobs that shook her with his body. "Oh God, sweetheart!" he whispered brokenly. "I'm so very sorry."

Chapter Eighteen

April 19

It had been less than two weeks since Paige had last been in her apartment in Mill Valley, but it seemed like a lifetime. So much had happened. So much had changed.

She knew now what Matt had meant when he'd advised her to let go. She knew he'd recognized that she had to acknowledge her grief before she could finish with it.

She had set out for Santa Barbara with such high hopes, and now those hopes were shattered. But the awful finality of that loss was not nearly as crushing as the loss of her marriage—the loss of Matt.

She sat numbly on the studio couch and watched Matt as he prowled around the apartment. He paused now and again to read the titles of the books on the shelves, or to adjust the Kandinsky print she could never get to hang straight, or to admire the butterfly mobile she'd made to echo the floral print of sunny yellow and dramatic aubergine with which she had covered the floor cushions.

Her apartment was a drafty, barnlike room that she had converted from the loft of what had once been a commercial building. When she'd first seen it, she had been entranced with its spaciousness and its profusion of funny old windows. After having lived all her life in the overfurnished stuffiness of her Aunt Rachel's house, the diminutive rooms of the modern apartments she'd looked at had made her feel closed-in, so she had jumped at the chance to lease this place.

She'd painted the walls off-white to make the apartment seem even larger than it was, and except for walling off the bathroom, she hadn't installed any partitions. She had used room dividers and furniture groupings to designate the various living areas. Over the years of her tenancy, she had furnished it sparingly with white wicker pieces, and filled it with plants and sunshine.

She had been contented here, but now she looked about critically, trying to see the apartment as Matt might, and it struck her that she had been deceiving herself in thinking she had created a home that was bright and roomy. In her present mood, it didn't seem cheerful at all. It seemed stark and barren.

At last Matt nodded, as if he were satisfied with what her apartment revealed about her. As he sat beside her on the couch, he said softly, "So this is where you've been living. It's like you, Irish. It dares to be different."

Paige choked back a sob and replied in a cracked whisper, "Sometimes a little too different."

"Maybe sometimes," Matt agreed.

When he smiled at her, she thought she saw a hint of tenderness in his smile. Telling herself her eyes must be playing tricks on her, she quickly looked away from him, leaned her head against the back of the couch, and closed her eyes.

"You were right, Matt," she said woodenly, "about so many things."

"For instance?"

"I—I was a rebel...."

"You still are!"

"And there is safety in numbers...."

"Ah, but given the right people, two can be the safest number of all."

She thought she heard laughter in his voice. Was he mocking her? "And your feet do get covered with tar on the beaches in Santa Barbara...."

"As long as it's only your feet, who gives a damn?"

This time the levity in his voice was too blatant to be ignored. She opened her eyes to glare at him, but her expression softened when she saw the way he was looking at her. He did appear to be amused, but there was something else....

"You were right about my search, too," she said flatly. "It was a wild goose chase."

"Was it?" he asked gently. "I disagree with you on that one. At the outset, you told me it was something you needed to do, and I could see that it was."

"All right," she admitted, "you're right about that

as well, but you were wrong about one thing. I may have lied to myself, but I never lied to you."

"No, I know you didn't, and that's another reason why this hasn't been a wild goose chase. Stella told me something...."

"I thought she must have, but I really don't recall ever discussing you with her."

"How about your aunt? Did she know about us?"

"I'm not sure. I suppose she might have guessed. I mean—well, you did come to Alder Creek to see me that day."

Matt nodded thoughtfully. "I think we can safely assume that she knew I was the father of your child. And I think we can also assume that she saw me as representing a greater threat to her plans for your future than your pregnancy ever did."

Completely bewildered, Paige stammered, "H-how can you be so certain of that?"

"For the simple reason that Stella told me you'd never received my letters."

"You wrote to me?"

"Several times. I stopped writing when I didn't get any letters in return."

Smiling, Matt slipped his arm around her with an easy indolence that demonstrated how confident he was that she would not resist him.

"Please don't," she protested feebly when he pressed her head into the curve of his shoulder and rested his cheek against her hair. "I can't think when you do that."

"I don't want you to think. I just want to make love

to you." His arm tightened about her, holding her even closer. "But first, I'd like you to answer a question or two."

"I—I'll try to," she conceded breathlessly.

With barely concealed urgency, he asked, "Is it too late for us? Is that why you suddenly became so blasted remote last night?"

"Oh, Matt, I don't know if it's too late, but I acted the way I did last night because I was jealous."

"Jealous?" he repeated sharply. "But why? Is it that you don't trust me?"

"I trust you, but I don't trust Cynthia Waring. She's in love with you, Matt."

"Is she?" Matt was taken aback. An embarrassed flush darkened his face. "For Pete's sake, Irish," he muttered, "I know Cynthia's attracted to me physically, but I'd hardly call what she feels for me love!"

"Well, I would. And besides, I saw the way you were kissing her hand at the party the other night—"

"I meant for you to see it," Matt said evenly.

Outraged by his confession, Paige tried to pull away from him, but he wound his other arm around her and refused to release her. Her struggles stopped the moment he disclosed, "I only did it because I was jealous when you came in with Derek What's-his-name. But all that was days ago, Irish. Something must have happened since then to set you off."

"Something did," Paige replied. "Cynthia paid me a call yesterday afternoon. She said she'd come by to pick up some of her things, but I think mainly she wanted to gloat because she has a key to your house and I don't."

"That's easy enough to explain," said Matt. "I don't know whether she actually came to get something that belongs to her, but I gave Cynthia a key so she could come and go as she pleased when she was overseeing the contractors who did the remodeling in the house. When the work was done, I forgot to get it back."

"Then you weren't with Cynthia last night?"

"Lord no! I drove around for a while, then I stopped by Joe's."

From Matt's response, it was obvious that Cynthia was the last person he'd wanted to be with, and Paige sighed, relieved to be able to put that worry behind her. But there was still the matter of the perfume.

"I don't know what gets into Cynthia sometimes," Matt continued as if he'd read her mind. "For a woman who's usually the picture of grace, there are moments when she can be the world's worst klutz. She gave me a hard time yesterday too, bugging me about what she should give you for a wedding gift. Her motives might have been unselfish, but she made a royal pest of herself! She phoned several times and she came to the office twice. The second time she was showing me this perfume she wanted my opinion about, and she wound up spilling most of the stuff on me!"

Paige swallowed a giggle. "What a nuisance for you," she remarked with mock solemnity. Arching toward Matt, she planted a kiss on his chin and prompted, "Next question."

"There's just one more," he replied. "Why wouldn't you marry me when I asked you to eight years ago?"

"Because, like you, I can't take being tolerated. After the way you used to talk about marriage, I knew you'd proposed simply because you wanted to do the decent thing by me, and I'd had enough of being a burden with my aunt. I didn't want to go from being her responsibility to being yours."

Matt stiffened with surprise. For long moments he was silent. "Stella said you called for me when the baby came. And afterwards, when you were so sick."

"Really, Matt! You can hardly hold me accountable for whatever I might have said when I was delirious—"

"Can it, Irish!" Matt growled repressively. "There are occasions when I find your talent for dodging issues entertaining. Sometimes it's a regular laughriot, but this isn't one of them."

Acknowledging defeat, Paige allowed her body to go slack. She relaxed against Matt and buried her face in the warm hollow of his neck.

"I told you I hadn't lied about loving you," she cried. "Oh, Matt, I loved you so much. I would have given almost anything to marry you. But I couldn't have borne your marrying me just to do what you saw as your duty."

"And that's it?" Matt asked incredulously. He gripped her upper arms and held her away from him so that he could see her face. His eyes were merciless, fiery with some hot inner light as they raked over her features.

"Irish, is that *all* that's kept us apart all these years?"

Paige lifted her chin proudly. "Maybe it doesn't seem like much of a reason to you, but it was terribly important to me. It still is."

Before she could object, Matt had pulled her into his arms and was holding her with a ferocious ardor that seemed to defy everyone and everything that might try to separate them again.

"You darling little dope," he muttered. "Didn't you know that I loved you too? Didn't you know that all my antimarriage talk was just a stupid effort on my part to convince myself I didn't love you, that I didn't want to marry you?

"I loved you so much, wanted you so much, I couldn't see straight, much less think straight. But you were so bright and lovely and gifted, and you had years of school ahead of you. And if that wasn't enough, you'd had so damned little experience with men. I knew you had a crush on me, but I felt like a cradle-robber. I didn't see how I could ask you to tie yourself down before you'd had the chance to play the field for a while.

"Then, after the night we were together, I couldn't kid myself any longer. That day I came to see you in Alder Creek, I was *praying* you were pregnant. I thought if you were pregnant, you'd *have* to marry me."

"B-but you loved being free and traveling all over the world," she argued dazedly. "What about your dream of finding the one country that deserved the color it was assigned on the map in the geography text?"

Matt shouted with laughter. "Irish, sweetheart! I always knew you were gullible, but surely you didn't take that seriously."

When Paige tilted her head back into his shoulder and stared up at him in amazement, he saw that she had taken him seriously, and he said, "I have to admit, the reason I traveled was nearly as fantastic as that, but it wasn't anywhere near as romantic."

"Then why—"

"It was an escape, that's all. The way I had it figured, if I didn't stay in one place for any length of time, that gave me a plausible excuse for not being close to anyone."

"But you had so many friends!"

"No, Irish. I knew lots of people. I had a lot of acquaintances. But until I found you, I never had any real friends."

"Oh, Matt—" The rest of what she'd been about to say suddenly seemed unimportant when Matt silenced her with a kiss.

His lips hovered sensuously over hers as he murmured, "My darling, Irish, you're the sunshine of my life. You're my best friend, my lover, and my wife, but there are times when you talk too damned much."

Taking Matt's sweet admonition to heart, Paige happily remained silent. They had plenty of time for explanations. They had all the rest of their lives, so instead of talking, she kissed him with all the tenderness and passion she possessed, and let her body tell him how deeply, how thoroughly, how wantonly, she loved him.

Just before dusk, when the last rays of sunlight found their way into the apartment, Matt gazed at Paige as she lay in his arms. She was delectably tousled and flushed with fulfillment. Her body was curled pliantly into his, and she was bathed by the clear golden light until he was dazzled by her radiance.

"You are so beautiful!" he whispered roughly. "I'm sorry we can't take a wedding trip just now. I'd like to show you Majorca or Capri, but I have to be back in Santa Barbara for a business meeting the day after tomorrow, so we don't even have time for a trip to Catalina."

"It doesn't matter," Paige said lightly.

"Still," he mused as if she'd tried to argue the point, "it would be a waste to travel to some exotic faraway place and spend the whole time in bed when there's a perfectly good bed waiting for us at home."

He ran his marveling fingertips over her breasts, along her rib cage to her waist, and over the satiny skin of her abdomen. He felt the response that rippled through her, and his voice was husky with desire as he said, "Maybe in thirty years or so we'll be ready for a honeymoon."

"I really don't mind," she replied dreamily. "I'm rather eager to get back to Santa Barbara myself." Throwing her arms around his neck, she pulled his head down to hers and murmured, "I have some important business of my own to transact with a lovely little goddess by the name of *Kuan Yin*!"

"You're too late, sweetheart." The velvety timbre of Matt's voice was enriched by his meaningful laugh. His hands moved with eloquent intimacy in loving exploration of her body as he said, "Since you've taught me the dangers of leaving anything to chance, I've already placed our order."

Yours FREE, with a home subscription to SUPERROMANCE ™.

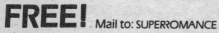

Complete and mail
the coupon below today!
